The Monster of Deep Water Lake

This is a work of fiction.
Names, characters, businesses, organizations, places, events, and incidents are either products of the author's imagination, or are used fictiously. Any resemblance to actual events, locales, organizations, or persons (living or dead) is entirely coincidental.

Copyright © 2021 Killarney Traynor and Margaret Traynor
Copyright © 2023 by Killarney Traynor

All rights reserved. No part of this book may be reproduced in any manner whatsoever without written permission except in the case of brief quotations embodied in critical articles and reviews.

First Printing, 2023

Cover by MiblArt

The Monster of Deep Water Lake

Encounter Series: Book 3

Killarney Traynor

Margaret Traynor

Original Thirteen Publishing

*I must go down to the seas again, to the lonely sea and the sky,
And all I ask is a tall ship and a star to steer her by;
And the wheel's kick and the wind's song and the white sail's shaking,
And a grey mist on the sea's face, and a grey dawn breaking.*
-John Masefield

Charles Emery, *Chief Petty Officer in the US Navy*

Captain Harry Donovan, *a former salt-water fisherman*

Norah Donavan, *his daughter*

Sherriff Young, *the local law enforcer*

Philip Cabot, *Donovan's nephew*

Article

THE MONSTER OF DEEP WATER LAKE

The lake resort town of Deep Water, NH, may just become the next Loch Ness. A local man reported having been attacked while night fishing by a monster – and claims he can prove it.

Captain Harry Donovan, formerly a fisherman from Portsmouth, was out on Deep Water Lake by himself Tuesday night when he claims something attacked his boat and tried to flip it. Donovan fought off his attacker and collapsed with a heart attack. He was found by his daughter, Norah Donovan, still in the boat, at dawn.

When asked to describe his attacker, Donovan denied that it was a man or even a merman, saying that he couldn't see much by moonlight, except that it had teeth or claws.

While his arm was sliced up in a manner consistent with his story, local authorities are not crediting the wound to a lake monster. Donovan had been drinking the night of his alleged attack and Sheriff Roger Young believes the cuts are attributable to a drunken accident.

"Men cut themselves on fishing lines all the time," Young said. "They don't all blame it on monsters."

Donovan is home now and insists that, not only was he attacked, but that others have been as well and that his boat bears the scars of the attack. Sheriff Young and his deputy escorted Donovan back to his house and examined the evidence.

"His boat is scarred," Young said to this reporter. "But he might just as well have run aground as anything else." When asked if the sheriff was considering issuing an official warning to would-be swimmers and fishermen, Young responded, "Absolutely not. Deep Water Lake is safe. There are no monsters. Any child knows that."

Meanwhile, local merchants and hoteliers are concerned about the effects this wild accusation will have on their business.

"People won't fish where there are monsters," Thomas Murphy of Murphy's Bait and Tackle said *when interviewed. "This could ruin us. This economy is bad enough. A rumor like this could finish Deep Water for good."*

"People are frightened enough already in these hard times," added Mrs. Smith of Cheshire Road. "We don't need imaginary creatures making it worse."

Deep Water is a resort town and most of the citizen's income comes from tourists. With hard times affecting everyone, business is already down as people are less inclined to go on vacation. When asked if the thrill of monster hunting might lure the curious rather than drive them away, Mr. Murphy said, "People come here to relax, to fish, to swim. They aren't going to bring their families to a dangerous area." He added, "The real tragedy in this story isn't that a man got drunk and saw something at night. It's that his vision might bring ruin on this town. I don't know how folks are going to react to that."

Is there a monster in the lake? It seems unlikely. But for Captain Donovan, who has since ceased talking to the press, the world has gotten a lot darker.

Part 1: The Fisherman's Tale

t was a brilliantly bright day the afternoon that Chief Petty Officer Charles Emery rolled into Deep Water, New Hampshire, in his borrowed Model A Ford. The sun was high in a cloudless sky, the roads were clear of almost all traffic, and the White Mountains looked as grand as the Alps in the background. When Emery stopped on the side of the road to stretch his legs and grab a quick smoke, he noted the pure quality of the air. The salty brine scented air of the Atlantic had been replaced with spicy pine and the grounding scent of dirt. He wasn't quite sure if he liked the substitution.

His stopping point was an overlook of the town and he examined it as he worked his way through his cigarette. Deep Water was one of those lake resort towns which had sprung up during the gay nineties, withered during the Great War, revived in the twenties, and was struggling again in the wake of the Wall Street Crash. From a distance, it looked peaceful and pretty, like a post card, and one could be forgiven for thinking all was as it had been. But Emery had learned not to trust outward appearances. It would be hurting, like all towns in the country were hurting, but it was going to great lengths to disguise the wound.

Charles Emery was a romantic in his way. As a small child, he'd yielded to the siren song of the sea and as a youth, he'd answered the call of his country, lying about his age in order to qualify. When the epidemic of 1918 stripped him of all reason to come home, he'd stayed in the Navy. During that time and in the intervening years, he felt that his career was all about protecting the country he loved from outside forces, only to find that an inner rot had done more damage than the Kaiser ever could have. Now, twenty years later, retirement was staring him in the face and for the first time in his adult life, he didn't have a direction.

"Times are changing, Charles. The navy is moving in a new direction and needs new ideas."

Times *were* changing. Things had slowed and tightened after the crash of '29 and the disarmament treaties that followed. The scuttlebutt was that sailors were on their way out. Aviation was the rule of the day. In only a short time, the *Ranger* would be launched, the first ship of its kind, designed specifically as an aircraft carrier. The Navy, it would seem, would be regulated to escorting the US Army Air Force. The old seaman was becoming a thing of the past.

Yes, times were changing and yet Emery had not. The idea of a desk job, a training position or, worse still, retirement, filled him with an existential dread that he couldn't shake. His passion was for the sea, his work the Navy. He'd risen through the ranks to become Chief Petty Officer and his life had been one filled with responsibility and solid work. Without family, without ties to the mainland, the sea had become his life. Without the Navy, he didn't know who he was.

His superior, when discussing Emery's career options, had not helped: *"You should take retire-*

ment. You've got a lot of useful years ahead of you. You should do something new, something different."

His usual inner calm had fled at that thought. So when the letter from Deep Water came, Emery had jumped on the chance to get a change of scenery and maybe perspective.

Now, he leaned against the Ford, lifting his face to the sun and letting its warmth drench him through. Behind him, another automobile chugged along the winding road, disturbing the air with sound and exhaust. He ignored it and allowed the sound of the birds and the trees rustling overhead scrub away at his inner turmoil.

Twenty years in the Navy, he thought. *Twenty years and what have you to show for it?*

There were no answers in the wind and the sun. He flicked his cigarette stub away and climbed back into the Ford.

2

It was a short drive into town and Emery was hungry by the time he got there. His original estimation had not been wrong. Deep Water looked battered and worn. The streets were subdued, even for a resort town at the beginning of the season, and the houses looked as though they could use a coat or two more of paint. Men lounged in the streets, watching as his car drove by. One boy gave him a thumbs up for the car. Emery nodded in appreciation. The Ford was a few years old, but Manny kept it in great shape and insisted on giving it an extra coat of polish before he loaned it to Emery.

"Can't have my old Chief drive around in a smudgy car," he'd said.

Emery had appreciated his consideration, but

looking around the near-deserted streets with their dusty, neglected cars, he wondered if he hadn't made a tactical error. No one would overlook his arrival now.

A diner came into sight and next to it was a gas station. Emery pulled in and was glad to give the bored attendant some business. He left the man filling the tank and checking the oil and water and walked into the diner.

The lunch rush was over, if there had been such a thing, and the place was nearly deserted. A few men sat at the bar, nursing their drinks or finishing bowls of thin soup. One group was huddled around a newspaper, talking in low, excited tones. As Emery took his seat, it occurred to him that he hadn't seen the morning paper.

The waitress was a thin woman with frizzy red hair and a sunburnt face. She poured him a cup of coffee as she asked what he wanted.

"A burger, if you have it."

"Coming up," she replied and called the order into the kitchen. Then she slid the cup in front of him. "Staying in town or passing through?"

"Just visiting," he said. "You wouldn't happen to have a spare newspaper around, would you?"

"You can have Joe's when he's done." The waitress jerked her head towards the men at the end of the bar before she moved off to fill someone else's cup.

Despite the warm day, the diner was chilly and dark. Emery sipped his coffee, which was hot, bitter, and a little thin for his taste. People were cutting back everywhere, even in coffee beans. He ignored the curious glances he was generating and reached into his pocket for his notebook. Tucked inside was the letter that had brought him to Deep Water, a ragged piece of paper that was little more than a note written in a shaky, elderly script. Despite the degeneration of the hand, he knew the writing well.

He read it, and then reread it, but the letter made less sense than before. All that was plain was the plea: *"You are the only man I can trust... I can think of no one else to turn to."*

My old friend, how much did it cost you to write this?

"Here's your sandwich."

The waitress's cheery voice cut through his musings. She thumped a heavy plate in front of him, filled with a charbroiled burger on a whitened bun, a dill pickle lolling next to it. "Need anything else?"

"No." Emery hastily tucked the letter back into the book and the book back into his pocket. "Actually, salt and pepper and ketchup if you have it."

"You got it, Sugar."

The door slammed open behind him. Emery turned.

A tall man, heavily built and wearing worn jeans and an untucked shirt, strode into the restaurant, battered hat in hand. His gaze passed over Emery and landed on the group of men with the newspaper. He seemed about to approach the bar when his gaze landed on the headlines. His face tightened.

The man with the paper looked up and smiled, but there was something malicious in the manner with which he both smiled and waved the paper in greeting.

"Morning, Tom!" he said, cheerfully. "How's it going?"

Tom was not in the mood for cheerful greetings.

"Damn that Jones," he spat out. He strode over and ripped the newspaper out of the man's hand. He held it out in front of him, like he needed glasses, and squinted at the headlines. "Damn him! I told him to kill that story, before it killed us."

Emery twisted around in his chair and squinted at the headlines himself. He could only just make out: *WITNESS GOES SILENT ON DEEP WATER MONSTER STORY.*

The man who'd lost his paper seemed satisfied with his reaction. "Man's got to sell his papers, Tom," he said drily, leaning back against the counter and watching Tom with malicious eyes. "Hard times, these."

"And *he's* making them harder, Joe!" Tom slapped the paper. "Who's going to want to come here to fish? Who's going to bring their families up here to swim with *this* kind of thing going on?"

"Not like many were coming anyway," another man drawled.

"Well, they sure as hell aren't coming now!" Tom wadded up the paper in his fist and shook it. "Damned irresponsible. We have jobs we need to keep. Some of us won't make it through the winter if the season gets screwed up by these... these lies!"

"Take it easy, Tom," the waitress said.

"One crazy old man gets blind drunk and sees things." Joe shrugged. "Ain't no one going to believe him. Heck, a lake monster might liven things up some!"

Behind Emery, the door swung gently open. A man wearing a sheriff's badge stepped almost silently into the diner, hat in hand, his small dark eyes on the group of arguing men. He was a large man, one who ate a little too well, but he carried himself with an earned authority that made Emery think he was not to be underestimated.

The sheriff glanced at Emery, sizing him up quickly before turning back to the commotion.

Tom threw the mangled paper to the floor and stepped closer to jab his finger into Joe's chest.

"You may laugh at this, Joe Barker, but mark my words. Word is going to get out and when it does, we'll be in trouble, real trouble. Dust bowl trouble. And it'll be their fault, that old man and Jones. I for one don't intend to lose my job because of a crazy old man and a lunatic newspaperman.

Someone ought to do something. Someone ought to run them out of town and teach them that you can't just say things and start trouble for people!"

"Seems like someone's already started doing that, Murphy."

The sheriff's voice rang throughout the diner. Tom started and whipped around, the color draining out of his face. The sheriff moved toward the bar, dropping his hat on the counter in front of a stool next to Emery.

"Someone already got to Donovan," he said, coolly leaning on the bar and looking into the startled Tom Murphy's face.

Emery stopped mid-bite. His mouth dried up and his appetite, hardly appeased, disappeared. He forced himself to lower the sandwich slowly, to keep his movements steady so as not to draw attention to himself. For all his care, the waitress gave him a curious look. Luckily, she was more interested in the sheriff than she was in a stranger.

The sheriff was enjoying himself. He took the proffered cup of coffee from the waitress with a nod and then went on laconically: "Yup. Funny thing about that old man. One minute, he's pulling kids out of the water and screaming at me to call in the state troopers, next moment he's holed up in his house, won't come out, won't speak, won't deny or confirm. Kinda strange, don't you think, Murphy?"

Tom licked his lips and shrugged. Joe Barker looked even more pleased.

"Maybe he finally came to his senses," Tom said. "Realized how crazy he sounded."

"Maybe," the sheriff admitted. "Maybe someone... convinced him. I don't suppose any of you would know anything about that."

He looked directly at Murphy as he said this and the temperamental Irishman turned beet red.

"Are you accusing me of something, Young?" he demanded.

"Now, Sheriff," Joe Barker said, in a conciliatory tone that Emery didn't trust in the least. "Tom here has a temper, but he's not exactly a gangster."

"I'll thank you to keep out of this, Joe." Sheriff Young kept his tone level and his eyes on Tom Murphy. "I'm not accusing anyone of anything. Far as I know, nothing happened at all. But seeing as you're a public spirited man, I'm just wondering if maybe you had a word or two with old man Donovan. Dropped the bug in his ear about the damage his crazy story would do to this town. You know... did what me and Deputy Boone couldn't do, bound by the law as we are."

Emery shifted in his seat. His grip on his coffee mug was so tight his knuckles were white. Young, alerted by the sound of his movement, tossed him a curious glance, then went right back to Tom.

"Well, Murphy," he said. "Did you speak to our friend Donovan recently? Maybe visit him? Maybe did more than talk to him? You know. In the heat of the moment?"

Tom was breathing heavily. His eyes darted from one face to another's as his face turned from white to red to white again.

"I haven't done *anything*," he protested, but his voice had lost power and he was nearly whispering. "*Nothing*, do you understand? Nothing to nobody."

The silence stretched out for a long, long minute. Then the sheriff leaned back and nodded.

"I'm glad to hear you say that, Murphy," he

said. "Real glad. I hated the thought." He slapped the counter and turned to the waitress, who was watching this exchange with her mouth open. "Minnie, how about some more coffee and a slice of that pie?"

Minnie moved to fulfill the request as an awkward silence descended on the diner. Tom Murphy looked as though he'd been cast adrift in the sea. He shifted in his stance, first towards Joe, then towards the bar, but a glance at the sheriff seemed to make up his mind. Rolling his battered hat in his hands, he slunk out the door, not even responding to Minnie's "Did you want something, Tom?" The door slammed behind him.

Joe whistled and the other men laughed and turned back to their paper. Sheriff Young made small talk with Minnie as she dished him up a plate of apple pie and threw a slice of cheese on it.

Emery picked at his half-eaten hamburger, but found he had no desire to remain indoors. He got up so abruptly that his movement alerted both Minnie and the sheriff.

"Thanks for the meal," he said, fishing some change out his pocket. "I think this will cover it."

He dropped the coins into her hand and grabbed his hat. Minnie glanced at the change before gulping up at him.

"You hardly touched your hamburger," she said.

"You in a hurry, mister?" the sheriff asked, with the same mock-friendliness he'd used on the other men.

"You could say that," Emery nodded to Minnie and was reaching for the door handle when Young spoke again.

"Staying here, friend?" he asked, in a tone that would not be ignored. "Or just passing through?"

"On my way to visit an old friend," Emery said.

"That's nice. Anyone I know?"

"I couldn't say." Emery smiled and was out the door before the sheriff could ask another question.

***

Tom Murphy had disappeared.

The station attendant was just lowering the hood on the car when Emery strode back up to him.

"You sure eat fast, mister," he said, cheerfully.

"Force of habit. You got a telephone?"

"Inside. You'll need a nickel."

"Fine. Give me a paper and add it to the tab."

"Right, boss!"

Emery found the phone and gave the instructions to the operator, but the phone rang with no answer. Emery slammed the phone back into its cradle and leaned on the desk for a long moment, trying to calm himself down. His temper was hot – he could feel the blood pulsing in his forehead.

"Someone already got to Donovan."

Damn it!

He refrained from pounding his fist into another man's wall and pulled himself together instead. When he regained his equilibrium, he drew himself up, straightened his suit, and then went out to pay his tab. While he did so, he saw Sheriff Young exit the diner, hat still in hand, squinting now against the sun. He stopped by the patrol car and scanned the area until his gaze fell on Emery.

Neither man nodded greeting. Emery paid the attendant and asked for directions. He jotted them down carefully in his little notebook, thanked the man, and got into his car. He was hardly on the road again when he saw that same attendant talking to the sheriff, no doubt telling him that the strange man with a military bearing and a sharp Ford had asked for directions to the Donovan house.

Dear Charles,

I have heard through the grapevine that you are coming into port on the 26th and that you'll be on shore leave for some time while your ship is in port. If you haven't made other plans, would you be willing to come up to my place in Deep Water? It's a nice enough town for a land-locked place, but there's also a lake full of fish waiting to be hooked. We have a spare bedroom and would be pleased to have you come and stay. More than that: I have a problem. A problem I cannot write about here, and I have no one to turn to. My daughter lives with me, but the problem is beyond her ken. You are the only man I can trust, now that my son is gone, and I can think of no one else to turn to.

If you can, please come.

Yours,

Donovan

PS: Please excuse the handwriting. My good arm was injured in an accident and I'm using my left.

"*...*h*oled up in his house, won't come out, won't speak, won't deny or confirm. Kinda strange, don't you think?"*

Sheriff Young's voice kept ringing in Emery's ears, making him grip the wheel tighter. The Ford was swift and nimble, whipping through the narrow, winding streets.

I should have come here sooner. I should have known something was really wrong. Donovan wouldn't have asked about something minor...

His memory went back when he was just a boy with too much time on his hands and Jeremy Donovan was encouraging him to come on a fishing trip.

"My dad's the best man on the water. We caught

a tuna once so big, it nearly capsized the boat! Come on, what else is there to do?"

It was an invitation Emery couldn't resist. He'd slipped out of his folk's house long before dawn that Saturday morning and found Jeremy waiting at the end of the street. They raced to the docks, where Donovan and his shipmate were readying the boat for a sail. Emery took one look at the powerful older man with the gray beard and thought, *Nothing can scare him.*

That was years ago. Before the Great War. Before the epidemic. Before the world went off its axis, first into prohibition, and then into depression. It was long, long before Donovan, born and bred on the waves, had given up the sea and retreated inland with his tail between his legs.

What could have happened to make Donovan give up the sea?

"I'm just wondering if maybe you had a word or two with old man Donovan... did what me and Deputy Boone couldn't do..."

Emery slammed on the accelerator and the car ate ground.

The directions the young man gave were simple

and clear, a good thing as the streets were indifferently marked. Emery drove the Ford through winding roads heavily overshadowed by tall pines, squat maples, and elegant birches. Squirrels raced across as though daring the Ford to run them down. The few farms were rugged affairs with rocky fields carved out of forest and manned by a man in a beaten tractor or on a worn horse.

When the tree line broke abruptly, the lake appeared again, shimmering in the afternoon sun, a relief from the unrelenting claustrophobia of the overhanging trees. Emery breathed easier near the water and wondered, again, what would have driven an old seaman like Donovan to leave the ocean behind for such a small, cramped space.

The road turned northwest and Emery followed it. Smaller houses replaced the farms now, cottages mostly rented by tourists and vacationing families. They appeared empty, but then, it was early in the season.

The road wound further and further and finally, just when Emery was starting to feel as though it would never end, the trees cleared again and there was the house.

It was a large place, with plenty of windows, dark wooden siding and a white trim that looked as though it had been freshly touched up. A covered porch wrapped around the front of the house, around the side and probably extended in the back as well. A wide gravel driveway led up to the front door and there was a carriage shed off to one side, where a wood pile and an ax spoke of recent activity. A bicycle leaned on the other side of the shed near an overturned boat with a scarred bottom and a well-used outboard motor. Beyond the house, the lake sparkled. A few chickens, plucking at the gravel driveway, fled as he pulled in.

Emery hopped out of the car and took in his surroundings. Overhead, the leaves rustled, trees creaked, and the water made gentle lapping sounds. Chickens clucked. Birds sang. But there was nothing else.

Emery shut the door and looked to the boat again. It was upside down, but he could make out the lettering: the *Daisy Jane*.

This was Donovan's house all right. Emery took the porch stairs two at a time and rapped on the door.

"Captain?" he called. "Captain Donovan?"

He waited for an answer, noting, as he scanned the yard again, that the large mail box at the end of the drive had its flag up and that the large number painted on the side was the same as the address on Donovan's letter.

"...holed up in his house, won't come out, won't speak..."

Emery rapped again, but still there was no answer. He stepped back and looked up at the upper story windows. No life fluttered there. He followed the porch around to the back the house. The porch itself was neatly swept and populated with weather-worn furniture. It broadened in the back and opened to a patio with a grill and a picnic table. The backyard was wide and cleared of trees. The lake lapped at the rocky shoreline and a weathered dock extended out into the water. A rowboat lay tied up to the dock, and on the shore, under a tall pine, a canoe lay face down on the pine-strewn ground.

Emery knew from maps that Deep Water Lake was kidney-shaped and loosely connected to a chain of lakes in the area. Unlike the resort cottages,

Donovan's land was private, framed on his side of the lake by dense woods laced with footpaths. The opposite shore was actually an island, forested but too small and too remote to build on.

He took all of this detail in as he walked around the house, but took no time to dwell on it. He seized the handle of the back screened door and yanked it open to knock on the windowed wooden back door. He knocked three times, then shaded his eyes and peered through the window.

The door lead into a kitchen and eating area. A man with silver hair lay slumped over the kitchen table with a bottle at his head. His right arm lay on the table, his sleeve riding just high enough to expose the bandages.

"Donovan!"

Emery grabbed the door handle, fully prepared to break the door down, but it gave readily. He stumbled into the darkened room, preparing himself for the worst.

"Captain..."

A gentle snore filled the silence. The shoulders, shrunken since Emery had last seen them, were rising and falling with regularity. The captain was not dead, as he'd feared. If the bottle's label was to be believed, he was merely dead drunk.

With a glance behind him, Emery gently shut the door, and then walked quietly around the table, examining his old mentor.

Captain Donovan was no longer the strapping specimen of a man he once was. His worn work-wear hung loose on his now-boney frame. The trim grey beard was now white and shaggy, as was his hair. His face was loose and peaceful in sleep, and free from bruising or any other signs of 'persuasion'. Time had shrunken the cheeks and hollowed the eyes. His hands looked the same though: calloused and big, one wrapped around the bottle and the other spread on the table.

Emery felt more than a little foolish. The talk at the diner had left him with an impression better suited to tough-guy detective novels and here he was, breaking in like he was Sam Spade or something. It was a stupid thing to do, but at least no one had seen him do it. And for the moment, Captain Donovan seemed all right.

He dropped his hat on the table and ran a hand through his short-cropped, curling hair.

Emery, your temper is going to get the better of you some day.

Donovan snored and Emery wasn't disposed to wake him yet. He took a look around the room instead.

The interior of the house was very simply styled and featured mostly wood paneling, obviously designed for holidays and not extended stays. The signs of America's economic rise and fall were evident even here: the kitchen appliances had been updated about ten years ago. The rough-hewn round table and the sturdy chairs spoke of local artisanship. Newspapers, mail, and kitchen paraphernalia gave evidence to a place well-lived in.

He poked through the pile of magazines at the end of the counter and found *National Geographic*, *Field and Stream*, *Power Boating*, and, even more telling, issues of *Yachting* magazine, half of them open to pages describing trans-Atlantic travel.

You grounded yourself, but you still haven't lost the scent of sea air.

He heard the creak of the screen door just before a voice asked, in a tone heavy with suspicion: "What are you doing?"

Emery turned.

A woman stood outlined in the open doorway, with one hand poised on the door, the other gripping a sturdy walking stick. She was pretty enough, rail-thin with long brown hair rolled up in a bun and big brown boots that dwarfed her small figure. A reddish-brown dog stood beside her, big enough to come half-way up her leg and so well trained that it merely watched Emery, rather than bark and wake the sleeping fisherman. Both were eyeing him with unveiled suspicion.

"Who are you?" Emery asked.

The woman's eyes narrowed. "I think the better question is who you are and what you are doing here?" She stepped inside.

"You must be Norah Donovan, the captain's daughter."

Her scowl deepened. "I *know* who I am. What are you doing here? Who sent you?" Another expression crossed her face. "If you're a reporter..." Her grip on the walking stick tightened.

"I'm not a reporter, ma'am," he hastily interrupted. "I'm a friend." He pulled the letter from inside his jacket pocket and held it out to her.

"Chief Petty Officer Charles Emery. Your father invited me."

He handed her the letter, noting her skeptical expression and feeling rather foolish for responding to her in such a military fashion. She took the letter and read it as he watched. Donovan stirred, muttering in his sleep, and then subsided again. The dog sniffed the hand Emery offered him, cocked his head, and barked once.

"Quiet, Fido," Norah said, firmly. She looked up with impatience when Emery snickered. "What?"

He shrugged. "I just... never actually met someone with a dog named Fido."

"My father named him," she said stiffly. She folded the letter and handed it back. "It's my father's writing, but I don't know why he sent for you. He must have been drunk."

"Maybe," Emery said, slipping it back into his pocket. "But I was not and am not in a position to make that determination."

"But you *did* think that his invitation gave you permission to just walk in and start poking through our mail."

"I didn't mean to pry."

"Sure you didn't." She pointed her stick at him. "Look, I don't know what my father thought he was doing, but we don't need help. And we don't need charity, not from *any* source."

He looked around the well-kept house. "That's evident, ma'am."

"Why are you here, Chief Petty Officer Charles Emery? What *were* you hoping to find?"

She stood before him with her feet spread wide apart, fixing him with eyes so deep and dark that they momentarily took Emery's breath away. He didn't wonder at her suspicions or her clearly defensive posture – hadn't he just broken into a house on a fool's errand because of talk in town? But why would she assume charity? There was no reason to think that Donovan had called on him for a financial reason and, anyway, it seemed as though everyone in the country needed help in that department. Emery was struck again with the idea that he'd sailed away from one America and had returned to another one entirely. But mostly he was taken by her clear eyes and the way she stood as though she could take him with only a walking stick and a dog named Fido.

Maybe he shouldn't have come. But then again, he hadn't imagined the talk in the town today.

She was waiting for an answer, so he told her the simple truth.

"Your father saved my life, ma'am," he said. "I owe him."

There was a beat of silence, and then Norah raised her chin.

"I'm sure you're very grateful," she said quietly. "But I'm looking after him now. Go home, Chief."

Now he was beginning to wonder if she even had a clue about the danger they were in. Emery only had a taste of it in town today and that was enough.

"If it's all the same to you, ma'am," he said, and gestured towards Donovan, "but I'd rather wait to hear what he has to say."

His polite manner and attempt at a conciliatory smile only generated an annoyed response from his reluctant hostess. Luckily for Emery, at that moment, Donovan's snoring choked. Fido barked and the old man rose from his prone position, shaking his head clear.

"Norah?" he said, rubbing his eyes.

She snapped instantly to attend him.

"I'm here, Father." She put her walking stick aside, leaned over the table, and took the bottle out of his hand. "I'll take that. You know what the doctor said."

The old man shook his head again, then, blinking, he looked around the room. When his rheumy gray eyes fell upon Emery, they lit up and he started up from his chair.

"Charles!" he cried. He immediately fell back into his chair, groaning and rubbing his head, then his bandaged right arm. He looked no less pleased when he focused on Emery again. "Charles, you've come! After all these years..."

His happiness was infectious and Emery grinned in reply. He leaned on the table and ignored the stern look Norah was throwing his way from the kitchen. Despite her and despite the strangeness of the place and the hostility of the town, he came as close as he'd ever had to feeling like he'd come home.

"I've come, Captain," he said. "I came as soon as I got your letter."

As sudden as Donovan's happiness had come, it

melted away again. The old seaman leaned forward and took Emery's hand, a surprising gesture that Emery didn't recognize. The old man's strength had not been entirely lost in the intervening years - his grip was almost painful. But more painful still was the look on the old man's face: it was one of terror, like a lost man seizing on one last chance at going home.

"I sent for you, Charles," he said, his voice hoarse and breaking, "because you are the only man I'll believe when you tell me I'm crazy."

Article

Article in the Tri-Town News: May 1934

WITNESS GOES SILENT ON DEEP WA-TER MONSTER STORY.

The witness who claimed to have been attacked by a sea monster these past few weeks has refused to give any further statements to the press or the police.

Captain Donovan, formerly of Portsmouth, reported that his fishing boat was attacked several weeks ago by an unknown lake monster. He further claimed that Horace Williams, a local handyman, was also attacked a week later, but Mr. Williams denied this charge.

"I was half asleep and was awakened by something rocking my boat," Mr. Williams explained. "It was odd, yes, but it wasn't an attack."

When local officials refused to take Donovan's claims seriously, Donovan tried to warn some of the locals, especially those with children on the water.

He was not believed and a scuffle broke out when he tried to prevent a boy from using one of the rental boats. Captain Donovan was given a warning by the police and told to keep his distance.

When asked by this reporter, Donovan's daughter, Miss Norah Donovan, explained that her father was still recovering from his heart attack several weeks ago and couldn't be disturbed. When asked about sea monsters, she refused to comment.

Despite police denials, rumors of a monster at the bottom of the lake persist, upsetting some of the locals. Some local businesses are worried about the effects of these rumors on business in a climate that already wasn't too promising.

Is there a monster in Deep Water Lake? The world may never know. But to quote one visitor, who'd decided against renting fishing gear during his trip this year, "Why risk it?"

efore Emery could respond, Norah interfered. She strode forward and removed Emery's hand from her father's grasp.

"Father, before we start talking about anything, you need to clean up for your guest. Now, go upstairs, wash and wake up."

Donovan agreed with practiced obedience, beaming at Emery as he pushed himself to his feet. "I'm just so glad to see you, Charles," he said again, as he reached under the table. "It's been so long. Stay, Fido!"

He pulled a cane out from under the table and leaned on it heavily as he moved towards the stairs. Emery had a hard time schooling the surprise out of his expression.

"Put on the coffee, Norah," Donovan said as

he limped off. "Give this man something to eat. Charles, we'll eat and talk old times."

"I'd be glad to, sir," he said.

Donovan went upstairs to do Norah's bidding and, surprisingly enough, she did his, making her displeasure known by banging pots and pans and slamming the water on and off. Emery amused himself by sitting down and playing with the dog, Fido, who proved friendly. Both of them jumped when Norah slammed the coffee mugs on the table in front of Emery.

"Do you need a hand, miss?" he asked.

"I can manage," she snapped.

When she turned back to kitchen, he couldn't resist asking, "Is there any milk?"

Her withering look spoke volumes.

"In the ice box," she said and slammed another pot.

Emery found it himself and bothered her no more.

When Donovan returned, he was standing straighter and using the cane much less. Frail as he was, frightened as he might have been, there was a surprising amount of strength and calm yet in

Donovan. Some of his years had peeled away and Emery saw, now, the remnants of the strong, cheerful, stubborn man who'd been his first mentor on the sea. His gray eyes weren't as sharp, perhaps, and there was a new touch of stoop in his back, but there was no doubt that he was the same man.

"Where are your bags?" he asked and there was a surprise clatter from Norah in the kitchen.

"In the car, sir," Emery replied calmly. "I haven't had a chance to stop at the hotel."

"Nonsense," Donovan snorted. "You're staying here. We have plenty of room."

"There's no need…"

"I insist. I dragged you all the way out here. The least I can do if offer you a room and board."

Emery looked over the old man's shoulder into the kitchen. Norah's back was towards them as she furiously cut at something on the counter.

Both men went out to the car to fetch the baggage. Being a service man, Emery traveled light. The one bag was soon installed in a small guest room on the second floor. Emery was struck by how clean and spare it was and was relieved that his window had a view of the water. The sun was sinking behind the trees. Several small boats, some sail, some motor-powered, lazily crisscrossed over the glittering waters. Despite his curiosity about the situation downstairs, Emery drank in the view like a parched man.

Donovan, leaning on his cane in the doorway with Fido at his side, said knowingly, "An old seaman can't stay far from the water, can he?"

Emery nodded, then turned.

"It's a poor substitute for the sea," he observed.

Donovan's smile faded and his right hand began nervously tapping his leg, a tic that Emery recognized.

"Why am I here, Captain?" he asked.

More hesitation, then: "Let's go downstairs," Donovan said. "Norah has the coffee ready."

And then there they all were, around the table, with steaming cups of Norah's coffee in their hands and slices of cheese and crackers in plates on the table. Norah sat across from Emery, silently sipping her coffee, her face wooden and unemotional. Donovan seemed to lose some of his energy, sinking into the chair as he fingered the rim of his cup. Fido curled up in a corner on a blanket by the unlit fireplace and lay watching the lake outside.

Emery's appetite had returned, sharpened by the scent of whatever Norah had going in the kitchen. He chewed through pieces of cheese with accompanying crackers and sipped his coffee black.

"I thought you wanted milk," Norah said.

He shrugged. "I was just trying to make conversation. Besides," he added, when her eyes grew narrow with anger, "this is too good to thin with milk. Far superior than what I had at the diner today."

She did not appear mollified, but Donovan said, "Hank's been watering his coffee down for years. He's a tight old man, isn't he, Norah?"

Norah shrugged. "He's careful," Her attitude said, "Let's get on with it."

Emery put his own cup down.

"All right, Captain," he said. "Suppose you tell me why you brought me down here today."

Captain Donovan looked into his cup, studying the liquid as though he could see some hidden message among the coffee grinds and cream. Then, as if gathering his courage, he put the cup down and reached behind him for the folded newspaper on the counter. Emery glanced at Norah, but she was intent on watching her father, her delicate fingers absently stroking her cup.

Donovan turned back to Emery and hesitated barely a moment before sliding the paper over towards him.

"I know you haven't had much time here in town," he said. "But I'm sure you've heard something about this."

Emery glanced down at the glaring headlines: *LOCAL MAN CLAIMS SEA MONSTER AT-TACKED HIS BOAT.* He took in the date, which was a week ago, and shook his head.

"I haven't seen this article," he said, scanning the print as he spoke. Words like *drunken accident* and *monsters* jumped out at him, along with another: *heart attack.* "I saw the follow up article today. You were in the hospital."

"He had a heart attack," Norah said, as though that explained everything. "He was very sick."

"Heart attacks don't cause hallucinations," Donovan said.

"Father..."

"Is that what this was?" Emery interrupted. "A hallucination brought on by drink?"

The silence that enveloped them was heavy.

Then Donovan said: "No."

Emery nodded. He pulled out his notebook and the pen that he always kept in his shirt pocket. He opened the book to a fresh page, checked the ink, and then looked at Donovan.

"Start from the beginning, sir," he said.

***

"This incident started a few weeks ago," Donovan said, rubbing his hand gently together as he spoke. "I'd gone with Jensen to help him pilot his new boat from the harbor up to Deep Water Lake. Jensen's a great fisherman, but he's a lake man – never had much experience on the ocean and the tidal river worried him. So I went along to help and…" He paused, shrugged, and continued: "I wanted to see the ocean again, get the salt in my nostrils. So I went and Jensen got his boat and then we took a spin out in the water, past Odiorne Point, into the waves. I hadn't been out there for so long it felt... big. Enormous. Like there was nothing but water and sky. I hadn't realized how much I'd missed it. But there was something else I felt while I was out there: I felt... watched."

"Watched?"

The old man nodded. "Watched. Well, anyway, we took to the river and began following it upstream, away from the ocean. But I still felt like someone was watching, following us. You know, that feeling you get when someone is staring at you but you haven't spotted them yet?"

"*Was* someone following you?"

Donovan's eyebrows went up. "Well, now," he said, softly. "That there is the whole question."

Emery shot a glance at Norah, but she was looking at her coffee mug, her mouth set in a tight line.

Donovan went on, "I lost that feeling once we left the Piscataqua River, and by the time we got to Deep Water, I was convinced that I'd imagined the whole thing. I'd been reading about the submarines and I thought, well, maybe there was one in the bay. We docked Jensen's boat with no trouble and I went home. A week later, we had the first incident."

"Which was?"

"Jensen's boat was vandalized. Someone scratched up the sides of it, like they were trying to climb on board and had knives for fingers."

Norah said, "We've had some vagrants in the area, stealing food and frightening people. There's a train station in town and they migrate up from Florida with the season."

She spoke as though she were talking about birds or some other regular migratory creature.

Emery nodded slowly. "Why would hobos knife up someone's boat?"

Norah's mouth tightened with displeasure.

Donovan said, "That's what I asked, but there seemed to be no other explanation. Like Norah says, we've had some trouble with panhandlers, but nothing more violent than a drunken brawl. We stopped asking questions and I didn't think any more about it. Then, one night, I decided to go night fishing. Billy Jensen was supposed to go with me, but his wife was poor, so I went alone."

Donovan leaned forward, his eyes on Emery, as though willing him to understand.

"I went out to the other side of the island,"

he said and his shoulders tightened as the story progressed. "It was a full moon and there were other boats on the lake, so I went to the far side of the island, to a place I know pretty well, where the fish are practically jumping into your boat. I set up there, near the island, in shallows. I laid out some line and waited. I had a bottle with me, so I was nursing that, of course. I was pretty tired that day – I'd worked at the Smiths, helping them with a roof – and I must have fallen asleep, because when I awoke, it was much later and something was bending my line."

His hands twisted into each other. His eyes had gone wide and were looking past Emery now, to the darkening lake beyond. There was an expression on his face, almost dreamlike – if that dream were a nightmare. But though what he saw in his mind's eye might have been terrifying, Donovan just kept telling the story, calmly, evenly, with practiced meter.

"An hour must have gone by. It had gotten cold. I grabbed the rod and bent-" here he hunched as though he were back in the boat, looking over the side "-over to try to catch a glimpse of the fish. That's when I saw him."

"Him?"

Emery leaned forward now and even Norah, who had been looking like she wished she were somewhere else, looked at her father with a frown.

The old fisherman shrugged. "Him. It. I don't know. A creature, not human, not animal. It had… limbs. And eyes – terrible eyes, watching me from just below the water. I could barely see him-it in the moonlight. It grabbed my line and pulled so hard I almost went over. I let go and fell back against the boat. Then it screamed… a terrible, terrible scream, like a panther or a banshee. It attacked my boat, tried to tip me over, grabbing at the sides, trying to get at me with its… claws or hands or whatever. The storm started then - I was half drunk and the rain was in my eyes. I couldn't think, I couldn't see. I grabbed an oar and I began to hit it and shout back. *Get off! It wasn't my fault! Get off!*"

Donovan's hands were gripping the table now and a thin sheen of sweat broke out on his forehead. Emery glanced at Norah and saw the same concern he felt on her face.

"I fought it, hitting it, hitting it with everything I had, screaming and screaming and screaming. It kept trying to climb up. It grabbed the oar and snapped it in two. It grabbed at my arm, ripped it. I panicked and stabbed it with the remnant. I heard a howl. The boat stopped rocking and then... it felt like my chest exploded. Everything went black. I thought, *this is it*. I thought I was dead."

"Father," Norah said gently and touched his shoulder.

Donovan started, as though he'd come out of hypnosis. He took a deep breath and suddenly seemed to realize where he was. His grip on the table was so tight, his knuckles were white. He released it, gave a half-hearted chuckle, and took a sip of coffee.

Emery gave him a moment before saying, "But you weren't dead. You came to."

"Yes," Donovan nodded. He absently rubbed his arm. "I came to. Somehow, I'd ended up back at our dock, shivering wet with a blanket on me, and Norah running out of the house. How I got there, I don't know. I just... don't know."

"His chest was black and blue," Norah said. "Like someone had pounded on him."

"Like chest compressions?" Emery said.

"Yes. But there was no one with him. He was bleeding badly, so I wrapped him up and called the Jensens. He came right away and we took him to the hospital. The next morning, we found that his boat was clawed up."

"Just like the Jensen boat," Donovan said and he leaned forward and jabbed his finger at Emery. "Someone or something *had* followed us up the Piscataqua. And it finally found me on my boat that night."

"A *creature*," Emery clarified gently. "A sea creature attacked your boat."

Under Emery's steady gaze, Donovan's confidence receded. He sagged against the back of his chair, an old man once again, and a tired one at that.

"That's what I thought happened," he said. "But it's not possible, is it?"

He looked so defeated, so strengthless that for a moment, Emery didn't know what to say. It was impossible and no one should believe a story like that. The man that Emery had known as a child wouldn't have. But he wouldn't have made it up, either. Like any good storyteller, Donovan was prone to exaggeration, but he was no liar and he didn't see things.

But then again, the man that Emery had known was a bold man of the sea, not the frightened fresh-water man before him. Something had happened to drive him away from the coast and, though the common explanation lay with the death of his beloved son, Emery had never quite believed that. Death happened and his boy hadn't died at sea.

Norah reached out and took her father's hand. She spoke to Emery even as she watched her father's face.

"The police came the next day," she said. "They examined the boat and decided that it was the act of a vandal or a vagrant. The official explanation is that my father was attacked by someone living on the island who wanted his boat."

"Did anyone search the island?" Emery asked.

"The very next day. I went with them. We found the remains of a campfire. Someone had been living there very recently, but they aren't living there now. It seems to support the sheriff's theory."

"Is that what you believe?"

She looked at him then. "If they'd wanted his boat enough to attack him with a knife, why didn't they take it when he collapsed?"

It was a good question. Emery looked down at his notes, which he'd written mostly without looking down. They didn't amount to much, just words or phrases that had jumped out at him while his mentor spoke. If anyone could decipher his handwriting, they would probably be puzzled at the collection, but Emery had long found it helpful to write as he listened. He retained more that way. Now he studied the words and slowly circled one phrase with his pen: *It wasn't my fault.*

"Have you seen the monster since?" he asked.

"No," Donovan said. "But I've heard it."

From the expression on Norah's face, this was news to her too.

"You've heard it?" Emery asked. "What does it sound like?"

"A wail. A... ghastly wail, like to make your insides go cold. I hear it and I know: he's still out there, looking for me, waiting for me." Donovan's eyes had gone glassy again and his face was paler than it had been a minute ago. "I haven't been on the water since." His voice dropped to a whisper, a whisper so low that both Norah and Emery had to lean into hear. "I shouldn't have gone. I shouldn't have risked the bay…"

"That's foolish, Father!" Norah said. "Why shouldn't you have gone?"

Donovan shook his head and closed his eyes.

"I don't know," he said softly. "It's just a feeling."

It was an unsatisfactory answer and Norah knew this as well as Emery. She opened her mouth to ask the next question, but Emery beat her to it with a question of his own: "Miss Donovan, do you hear the creature?"

She stopped, blinked, then shook her head. "No, this is the first I've heard about any sound. And he hasn't gone on the water since that night," she added, as though Emery needed further confirmation.

"How about the dog?"

"The dog?" She frowned.

"Does he hear the creature?"

"No," Donovan said. "I'm the only one. I'm... the only one."

There was another moment of silence, during which Emery circled the word *He*.

Then Donovan said, "It's true, isn't it? I'm crazy."

"What do you think?"

The old man held his gaze. "I must be. Sea monsters don't exist. You know that."

"I do." Emery searched his face and then shook his head. "But you don't." He closed his notebook with a snap and leaned forward with his forearms on the table.

Norah frowned in confusion, but Donovan simply waited for Emery to continue.

Emery said, "Captain, if you really believed you were crazy, you would have already turned yourself in to the authorities. But you didn't. Instead, you wrote to me, a man you haven't seen in ten years, and asked me to come and help you. You risked the wrath of the townspeople by insisting they stay away from the lake, even going so far as to try to stop a boy from taking a boat out. You challenged the law and even now that all of these are conspiring against you, you still hold out."

Donovan's eyes glittered.

"Aren't those signs of insanity?" he asked quietly. "A crazy man, staunchly averring that he sees monsters from the sea?"

He's too damn calm now, Emery thought, his temper flaring despite himself. *Too damn willing to accept this.*

"But you *are* questioning it," he said. "You're questioning it enough to write to me and..."

Impatience washed over him. He threw his pen down and jumped up from his chair to pace.

"What do you want me to say?" he growled. "I'm not a psychiatrist. I don't know the first thing about the human mind or how it works or how to tell when a man has lost it. I'm just a sailor, like you. I'm of no help."

He turned back to face him. "Why *did* you call me here, Captain?"

Donovan was watching him with that same expression on his face, the one that set Emery so ill at ease. It was the look of a drowning man who sees help arriving.

"I called you here," Donovan said, quietly, "because you're right. I don't think I'm crazy. I saw what I saw and I did what I did. But a *monster*..."

He leaned forward, his eyes bright. "Charles, if by some miracle I'm *not* crazy, then this town is in trouble. But if I didn't, then I'm..." He glanced at Norah then back at Emery. "Then I need you to tell me. Plain and clear. And do what needs to be done. Because despite what you say about me... I can't."

They stared at each other for a long moment. Emery saw a strange sort of calm in the old man, like he had, for the first time in a long time, recovered his sense of direction. He trusted Emery but what this meant...

Mental illness bore a nasty social stigma. If Donovan *was* really crazy and was found dangerous to boot – and it was likely a judge would find so in this case - then the captain would be sent to the asylum. Norah would bear the brunt of, not only the cost of his care if she didn't want him sent to a state facility, but the burden of being related to a man who'd gone crazy. Society assumed that mental illness was hereditary, which indeed it might be for all Emery knew, but society didn't believe in innocent until proven guilty. They would pity Norah – but they would cast her aside, just as they would her father.

Finding the man insane would wreak havoc on him and his daughter, possibly ruining both lives. But how could he *not* be crazy?

"You can't ask me to make that determination," Emery said. "I'm not a shrink."

"No," Donovan replied simply. "But you are the most honest man I know and you've never been afraid to speak the truth. And you will find the truth, no matter what that truth is."

When Emery still hesitated, he went on:

"I'm not asking you to act as my doctor. If I go to a psychologist, I know what they will tell me. But I *know* I was attacked and the creature is still out there." He shrugged. "But then again, crazy people don't know that they're crazy. I don't trust the doctors and the sheriff will not help. But if you tell me I was set upon by a hobo... Then I'll take my medicine like a man. But only if *you* tell me. Norah shields me too much. The others don't listen to me at all. You've never lied to me. I'm asking you to look into this. I'm asking you to tell me, to my face, what actually happened, if you can determine it. I'm asking you this as a friend… and because I have no one else to ask." He swallowed hard. "Please, Charles."

Emery stared at him hard for a moment, his stomach turning at the expression of faith in the old man's face. Then his gaze went to Norah. Her eyes told him nothing beyond what he already knew about her: she'd do anything to protect her father.

"I'm not a detective," Emery said at last.

"I know," Donovan nodded. "But you've always found the answers."

It was another way of saying that Emery was stubborn, almost to his detriment, a charge he freely admitted. But he also prided himself on being objective and thorough. Donovan was obviously in pain, emotionally as well as physically. Emery doubted he'd find anything more than the police had already determined. After all, who really believed in sea monsters? But if his looking into the matter meant that he could put the old man's mind at ease – and keep him out of harm's way where the locals were concerned – then it was time worth spending.

"I can stay a week," Emery said and turned away so he couldn't see the relief and gratitude that spread across his mentor's faith. "I can't guarantee a conclusion, but I can give you my opinion." He turned back to the table then. "Will that do?"

Donovan breathed a sigh of relief, looking as though a planet had rolled off of his shoulders.

"That will do," he said. "That will do very nicely."

There was a beat, and then Norah stood up. Emery noted the look of pained annoyance on her face. She didn't have her father's faith in his detective abilities.

Well, Emery thought wryly, *we have at least that in common.*

"I guess you'll be staying with us then," she stated and then began gathering the cups. "I'd better get back to making supper."

5

Norah didn't want help in the kitchen and judging from the look on her face, she didn't want any company at all.

Donovan, on the other hand, got up from his chair and asked Emery, "Where do we start?" He looked eager, as though they were the Hardy boys about to embark on an adventure.

Emery gathered his little notebook and pen and gestured towards the door. "Why don't you show me the scarring on the boat?"

Donovan agreed and they went outside. Fido followed them, romping around like they were on a picnic. The sun was falling behind the mountains now and the lake rippled quietly. Only a few boats disturbed the water and the peace of the early summer's evening. One motorboat zipped by, music blaring from a radio while a woman's drunken scream of mock-fear filled the air. Donovan winced at the sound, but didn't bother to look around.

"We have some money in this area," he said. His limp seemed more pronounced as they made their way across the pine-strewn grass. "They come up from the city for a few weeks every year, drink and party their way through the summer, and then disappear again."

"I'm surprised there aren't more accidents."

"It was worse during prohibition," Donovan said. "The neighboring town had a few watering holes and there's a club nearby. Out here in the boonies, no one bothered to hide it and we had a different sheriff then, one who liked to drink as much as anyone. Deep Water took a hit when they rescinded the law." After a moment, he added: "It'll take another if I'm right."

His face darkened with that thought and his strength seemed to leech out of him.

"Oh, I don't know," Emery said, lightly. "Loch Ness doesn't seem the worse for wear."

Emery wasn't known for his jokes and his delivery was so dry that it took Donovan a second before he understood. When he did, he chuckled and the depressing atmosphere dissipated somewhat.

"Here she is," he said, waving his free hand as they rounded the corner of the house and the up-turned boat came into view.

It was common enough for boats to have scars on their keels, either from rocks or from barnacles. But when Emery walked around the small fishing boat, he saw the difference immediately. The starboard side was relatively intact: it was the portside that had seen the action. There were scrapes, from minor paint chips to an actual gouge tearing up the side towards the rail. The rail itself was chipped and scored – Emery had to kneel to see the damage and when he ran his hand along the underside, he felt a divot, presumably where Donovan had stabbed his attacker.

"Was there any blood?" he asked.

Donovan shook his head. He was watching the lake now, as though on the alert. "We didn't find any. But then, there was the rain."

"Oh, that's right." Emery bent low to examine the wood more carefully. "You said it was raining."

"That was a funny thing. It was clear skies when

I went out – local forecast didn't say anything about rain. Yet when I woke, it was just getting ready to really storm. Stopped as soon as I came to afterwards."

"Rain bursts happen."

"Not around here, they don't," Donovan said firmly.

Emery didn't challenge that.

The party boat came back around the island, this time slowing down as they passed by the Donovan house. A drunken voice echoed across the lake: "Hey, Captain, where's the sea monster!"

There was a scream of laughter, both male and female, and then a roar of engine. Emery rose in time to take note of the boat and the tipsy nature of their driving. Then he saw that the old man was white again. He brushed his hands off and came around the boat to stand with him.

"Ignore them," Emery said and pulled out his cigarette case.

"It's getting harder to," Donovan admitted and took the proffered cigarette. "Thanks."

Emery took one for himself, then felt about for a lighter. "I thought you were a pipe man, Cap."

"I was. I am. But I take what I can get." He bent in towards Emery's lighter, then lifted his head and blew a cloud of smoke out into the yard. "Mind if I sit?"

"I'll join you," Emery said, lighting his own. "It's been a long day."

Donovan limped over towards the patio steps and lowered himself to face the lake. Emery leaned on the railing post and dragged deep on his cigarette. He could hear the faint sound of Bing Crosby crooning *Sweet and Lovely* drifting from the house. The sky was darkening and dusk was falling. The mosquitoes weren't bad yet, perhaps attributable to the breeze that came off the lake. Across the water, a few lights indicated where houses were, but for the most part, it was peaceful and quiet. Emery could almost understand why someone might choose to retreat here.

Donovan apparently thought so, too, because he breathed out another cloud of smoke and sighed. "It's something, isn't it?"

"Sure is," Emery agreed.

"You know why it's called Deep Water? It's technically the deepest fresh water in the state.

We've got one foot on Newfound Lake and the natives brag more about that one foot than I have anything I ever caught."

"Is that right?"

"Would I lie?"

"No, I reckon you wouldn't." After a beat, Emery asked, "Did Tom Murphy pay you a visit, Captain?"

He could feel Donovan grow tense beside him. "You know Tom?"

"I can't say that I do. The sheriff seemed to think he leaned on you and made you drop the monster story with the papers." Emery took another drag of his cigarette. "So did he?"

Slowly, reluctantly, Donovan muttered, "Yes. He did. But it wasn't anything, not really."

"Just words?"

"Stood on that porch and screamed at me. Told me I'd ruin the town if I kept talking, that I'd ruin him." Donovan looked at the cigarette in his hand. It was trembling now. "I'd never seen a man so scared, Charles. You'd have thought there *was* a monster."

"How worried are you about Murphy?"

Donovan seemed surprised by the question. "He's not a bad man. He's just frightened."

"Frightened, desperate men do terrible things."

"So have I. But I'm not worried about Tom and I don't think you should be either."

"As you say, Captain."

After a moment, Donovan said in a rush: "I don't know what frightens me more, Charles – a monster or the thought that I might actually *be* insane. Or the idea of being locked up in Whitcher Asylum, away from Norah, away from the water." He laughed bitterly. "If I wasn't insane, I think that would drive me to it."

"Captain, why haven't you told Norah the whole truth?"

Another moment of silence as the other man studied the lake. Emery could almost feel the reluctance rippling up Donovan's backbone. Finally, the old man said, "I told her everything about that night, just as I told you earlier. I haven't held anything back."

"And now you're lying to me. The fact of the matter is, this isn't the first time you've met this creature. It's the reason why you gave up the sea in the first place, isn't it?"

"Charles..." Donovan sighed.

"Lie to me, Captain, and I leave tomorrow. I owe you too much to do this job with my hands tied behind my back."

A moment passed. Bing Crosby faded to a jazzy tune, static ruining the jumpy beat. The scent of frying meat wafted out and surrounded them. Emery's stomach yawned open, but he wasn't about to abandon his opening now. He flicked his cigarette away, took a step forward, and then turned to face the Captain.

"*It wasn't my fault,*" he said and was pleased when the old man flinched. "Why would you say that to a creature you had never met before? Of all the boats that move up and down the Piscataqua, you expect me to believe you and Jensen were just randomly selected by this thing? My guess is you fought this creature before. And when you lost, you not only retreated, you gave up all together." He paused and then: "You gave up the *sea*, Donovan. Why would you do that?"

Donovan wasn't looking at him now. He was

staring at the ground, the cigarette burning low and forgotten in his hand. Fido, seeming to understand his master's stress, trotted over and laid his big head on the old man's knee.

Then Donovan said, "I was going to tell you but I... I was ashamed. And I couldn't. I should have known you'd catch it."

"It's better to sail straight into the storm than sideways," Emery said softly. "You taught me that."

He looked up then and his shoulders went back a little, even as his chin rose. "I did say that, didn't I?" he chuckled. "I thought I knew everything then."

"You did." Emery folded his arms. "Why don't you start at the beginning and tell me what *really* happened all those years ago?"

Donovan hesitated... and then he did.

Article in Portsmouth Crier, August 1925

FISHERMAN LOST IN A FREAK STORM

A freak storm off of the coast of New Hampshire had tragic results for a local fisherman. Captain Harry Donovan and Jasper Smith, both of Portsmouth, were fishing for sturgeon when an unexpected storm caught them unawares. Both seasoned seamen with a total of forty years' experience between them, they were nevertheless caught off-guard by the suddenness of the storm.

According to the police report, the two men had made a catch and were heading back to port when the storm caught them. While attempting to strap down the deck, Mr. Smith lost his footing in the sudden rain and fell overboard. Captain Donovan attempted to find him, but the storm made it impossible for a rescue.

"(The storm) came on like nothing I'd ever seen," said Thomas Mansfield, also of Portsmouth. His charter boat, the Merry Andrew, was filled with amateur fishermen when the storm hit. "We were tossed around quite a bit and there was some damage, but no one was really hurt. We lost a catch, though."

No charges are expected to be placed against Donovan.

"We are convinced that this was just an unfortunate accident," a representative of the Coast Guard said when asked for a comment. "Despite man's advancement, the sea is still a dangerous place and we do not expect that to change any time soon." When asked if there was any hope of recovering the body, the Coast Guard indicated that this was unlikely.

Donovan was not available for comment at the time of this printing. Mr. Smith leaves behind a wife and two children. Funeral services will be held at Immaculate Conception, the Catholic Church in Portsmouth, on Tuesday...

6

"We were out looking for sturgeon, Jasper and I," Donovan said.

He kept his voice low, as if even from that distance, he was afraid of Norah – or something else - overhearing him.

"It was night, of course. The sea was as still as a lake and the moon was enormous overhead. It was prohibition then. Jasper was a drinking man, like me, and he had this new batch of something he'd gotten from a friend of ours, homemade stuff, the kind that will peel paint off of the side of a barn. We'd worked our way through it during the day. I was drunk. I should have known better, but this outing was what I did. I could handle it and the hooch as well. Or so I thought.

"We'd pulled in a haul and I was exhausted and

ready to go in. But Jasper was determined to land a sturgeon. It was what we'd originally come out for and he had a hankering for 'black gold', he said, so we kept searching. You know what it's like, Charles. The still waters. The shimmering heat. The feeling that your prey is just below the surface, evading you, laughing at your attempts."

"I know," Emery said.

"We cast again and again and the night wore on. Just as I was about to tell him, that's it, we were going home, he said, 'Let's try the net.' So we did. And that's when we caught it..."

Donovan leaned forward, his eyes alit with excitement, as if he were seeing, again, the curve of the reel and hearing the slap of the water against the stern. Emery, who'd been on his fair share of such trips, found himself also in danger of falling back into memory.

"We knew it was big," Donovan said. "Damn near took the net out of our hands and it fought us every inch of the way. We pulled and we braced and we very nearly went overboard. Drink and network don't mix, I guess. But I felt *alive*, Charles. I felt alive and I knew Jasper did, too. We were going to make a killing, if only we could get that net into our boat.

"I don't know how we did it, but we did. We wrestled that thing on to the boat, inch by inch, until suddenly, the fish was over the side. It knocked us flat on our backsides. I was winded, but it was like Jasper had just found a vein of gold. He leaped back to his feet, laughing and shouting, *We've got it, we've got it, Harry!* And he grabbed that net to keep it from going back over board and then...

"Then he stopped laughing. Stopped moving. Stopped dead.

"I was laughing, lying on my back, looking at the sky. Clouds were gathering, blocking the moon and the stars, but I couldn't see the danger yet. I was too high on victory. 'Jasper,' I said, 'when we get back to town, I'm buying you a real drink!'

"He didn't answer me, not a word, not a grunt, not even a chuckle. I rolled over. I saw him, kneeling over the catch, still flopping on the deck, staring like he'd never seen such a sight before. So I took another look at it.

"And I stopped, too.

"I don't know if you've ever looked at those old books about mythology or monsters, Emery. I wasn't much into that stuff, but the kids, they liked it and I used to read to them from Grimm's and hero tales and the like. Those books always had drawings of the most grotesque creatures and I'd pulled enough creatures from the sea to realize where these artists had gotten their inspiration from. But I'd never seen anything like this. Never..."

"What was it?" Emery asked.

"A woman," Donovan's tone was dreamy and distant. "But not a woman. She had a woman's face and long tendrils where hair should be. She... shimmered in the starlight, like she had been formed from the water itself, droplets like diamonds against her skin. But her body... Scales and claws, a torso that was almost human and something like a tail. She was part fish, part human, a monster. She was the stuff of dreams and nightmares, and if a man looked at her too long, he'd be lost. Somehow I saw that. And I saw, too, that she was scared. She shook and whimpered, a low sort of musical sound. Like a siren. She was ugly, an abomination of woman and scale and claw, and yet she was… enchanting.

"And Jasper fell immediately.

"I was further away, you see, so whatever enchantment she had didn't work as strongly on me. But Jasper… he gaped at her, like a drowning man who sees his salvation. His voice, when he spoke to her, was low and crooning, like you would speak to a child. It frightened me, that sound, that look in his eye. Catching a monster was bad enough – but being trapped by one?

"I wanted nothing more than to throw her off of that boat and out of Jasper's reach. Or maybe him out of her reach? I don't know, except that I'd never been more frightened. And Jasper saw nothing but her."

He stopped then and looked at Emery.

"I don't expect you to believe me," he said and beneath the forced calm, his voice trembled. "I know you can't. But I saw her, Emery, and I saw what she was doing to Jasper. She was a siren, like in the tales, and we were heading for doom. I knew it. I saw it. I heard it. I tried to save him. I really did. But how can a mere man fight gods?"

He was growing panicked.

"Captain," Emery said gently. "What happened next?"

Donovan drew in a long breath.

"Jasper was already lost. He was touching her face, like a man in love, and it was then that I saw she was in pain. Our air wasn't good for her – she needed the water. She tried to tell Jasper – her claw grabbed his shirt and sliced through it like a knife through hot butter. But he couldn't hear her and he couldn't hear me. He just kept whispering over and over, *I've caught you. I've got you – you're mine.*

"'Jasper!' I said. 'She's dying! She has to go back in the water'

"But he couldn't hear me. Suddenly, I realized that it was beginning to rain. Somehow, despite it being clear only a moment before, a storm was whipping up. The sea began to churn. The very air was darkening, like an evil was closing in around us."

Donovan looked at Emery.

"I know it sounds melodramatic," he said. "But it *was* an evil. It wasn't natural, that storm. It was vengeful, like an attack. I felt it then, the darkness gathering around, trying to smother us. I *had* to get that woman off the boat and back into the water. We had to – to save ourselves as much as to save her.

"Jasper didn't notice. He was still crooning to the writhing woman, talking about taking her home where none else could have her, and she dying the whole time. I became desperate. I tried to pull Jasper off, but he fought me. He actually fought me and threw me backwards. I hit my head on... something, and while I was shaking off the stars, he grabbed his knife and stood over me.

"She's mine, Donovan, he said. His eyes were glossed over, like he was a crazed man. *You won't take her, she's mine!*

"'Jasper! You fool, release her, throw her back! She'll destroy us both!'

"He was going to kill me – and then... she found the strength to sing."

Donovan's face relaxed then. He was staring out into the water, as though he wasn't actually there, with Emery at all, but on a boat far away in the Atlantic, fighting for his life against super-natural forces. But now, he wasn't afraid – the enchantment of the old song rolled in on him and his eyes were soft, as though he were falling in love all over again.

"Oh," he whispered and there was heartbreak in the tone. "What a voice, Charles. It took your breath away. I've never heard the like before or since. Wordless and lovely, oh, so lovely, like a golden tapestry woven in the music of one voice. The devil's spawn could sing like an angel and we were hopelessly caught in its trap."

It was darker now. Overhead, bats flittered out like nocturnal butterflies, bobbing and darting in the cooling night air. Norah's radio took on a haunted sound of lovelorn jazz while, nearer at hand, a chorus of crickets competed with the sound of the water lapping against the shore and soft sounds of Fido's breathing. Emery was keenly aware of the gathering coolness and scent of smoke that clung to his own clothing.

Donovan seemed aware of nothing. He'd drifted off, back in time, and was lost in enchantment again. His hand lay still on Fido's back and his eyes were glazed and riveted on the water. He looked so far gone that Emery began to wonder if his initial judgement had been incorrect.

Then, with a start, Donovan came back and resumed his story, just as if he'd never paused it at all.

"She wasn't singing to us, of course," he said. "She was calling to her lover. Something snapped me out of the dream she'd frozen us in. I think it was the song itself – she was struggling still and her voice cracked, just enough to release me. The wind had kicked up and the waves, and the boat was in peril. I was – still am – more in love with my ship than any woman. I had to get her off my boat at once, to save it, to save us both. So I pushed Jasper back – kicked him. He fell and the knife went out of his hands.

"I got past him to the girl and I began pulling at the net. She was starting to choke, her song as choppy as the waves. She'd managed to snip some of the lines, so I pulled my knife and began to slash her free. I think she knew what I was trying to do, because she stopped fighting me. And then we both heard it."

"Heard what?"

"The reply," Donovan said. His tone went dry

with a fear as fresh as that night on the boat. "Her lover's answering call. It wasn't like hers. It was a howl of agony, of anger, of all the wicked things that had ever been converging on one spot. He had heard her and he was coming for her – for us.

"I panicked. I began to slice frantically, determined to throw her overboard in the net if I had to. His call came nearer and nearer – I was working as hard as I could –

"I forgot about Jasper.

"He tackled me from behind, knocking me off balance. My knife was gone. She screamed, but I couldn't do anything. He was a mad man. He kept hitting me, trying to choke the life out of me, even as the ship pitched and the storm raged and the monster came. I tried to knock him off of me, still trying to save his life and mine, but he was too far gone.

"She screamed again, weaker, and we both knew what it was: it was a death cry. Jasper stopped hitting me and we turned. She was writhing, looking more like a fish than a woman, but her agony was plain. My knife, the one I had been trying to cut her free with, was sticking out of her chest. It had slipped when Jasper tackled me.

"Jasper cried out and released me. He tried to save her, tried to pull the knife out, but it was too late – she was already... dissolving."

"Dissolving?" Emery interjected.

Donovan was shaking, the old horror still fresh. "She … started melting away. Like ice – snow on a sunny day. And the storm just kept roaring and the waves came higher. I heard *him*, again, bellowing his rage, roaring even over the storm, coming for us, getting nearer and nearer. I thought, if I could get her body into the water, he might be distracted and we might just have a chance.

"Jasper was bent over her, weeping like he'd lost a lover. I pulled him off and heaved what little remained her body over the side.

"But the net was caught on the hooks.

"I tried to free it and Jasper went mental again. He tried to fight me off, tried to pull her back on board. She was half in the water, still moaning, still dying. We fought, him weeping and me screaming, 'He's coming, you fool, we've *got* to get out of here!', but he couldn't hear me, wouldn't hear me.

"And then *he* was there – the... I don't know what you'd call him. A merman, a monster with scales and horns and claws, rising out of the raging sea like an avenging angel. He roared his fury again and this time, Jasper couldn't ignore him. I thought, *We're doomed*."

Donovan's expression contorted as though he were in real physical pain. Emery instinctively put out a hand, but stopped just short of touching him. He didn't want to break the spell, not until the story was over.

Donovan wailed in a whisper: "The monster saw her body and cried again, this time in pain. He grabbed her while she was still in the net and pulled..." A sharp intake of breath – this was painful. "Jasper cried, *No, she's mine, she's all mine!* He grabbed the net. I tried to stop him. I shouted, I reached, but the boat tipped and then..." His body sagged as though all the strength went out of it. "Then... he was gone."

"I heard Jasper scream one last time, an agonizing scream of terror and pain, like you'd never heard before. Then, it stopped, like someone ripped his lungs out. *His* cry took its place. It was...

triumphant and broken at the same time. Jasper was gone – I knew this. I... I cut the anchor, started the engine, and just drove off."

He sagged forward, burying his face into his hands, his voice becoming a wretched cry. "I left him there, Charles. I left Jasper."

A long moment stretched out between them. The captain's shoulders heaved with silent sobs. Fido whimpered and leaned on his master. Emery felt embarrassed. Donovan needed a moment of privacy, so Emery turned away, rubbing his face and feeling as though he'd just run through a minefield. The evening had almost completely faded into night now. The lights across the lake were like anchors, reminding him that he wasn't at sea, but very much inland, where they were almost always sure of someone's watchful eye.

When the captain's agony had softened, Emery turned back to him, pulling out the flask that he always kept in his pocket. He sauntered back over and offered his old mentor a drink.

To his surprise, Donovan waved it away and looked up at him instead. His face was in shadow, but Emery could almost hear the unspoken question.

"Have you told anyone else this story?" he asked. "Your wife, for instance?"

Donovan seemed to shrink again. He hesitated... and then nodded.

"I told her a modified version of the story," he said. "But I..."

"You began to doubt what you saw?" Emery asked.

Another hesitation, then, "Not... exactly. By the time I got into port, the booze had worn off and I thought... I thought, maybe there was something wrong with it. So when I docked, I went to the police. I had a contact in the police, and Paul Cabot, Sarah's brother. He always looked the other way when it came to the booze and he knew every cop and official in the district. I told him what happened. He didn't believe me, of course. He examined the boat, but there was nothing, no evidence, just shreds of the net. The... woman didn't bleed and Jasper had gone overboard and the hootch was gone too. There was nothing.

"The Coast Guard went around for a look, but

with the tides… When Jasper's body washed up a few weeks later, he'd been gotten at by fishes and there was very little left to him.

"I didn't know what to do. Neither did Sarah. So Cabot took charge. He thought that it was likely we had too much to drink, that maybe some of the moonshine was bad. When I insisted, he and Sarah sent me to a psychologist friend of theirs, a very discreet man with a practice in the mountains. We had Norah to think of, you see. She was young, still in school then and seeing a young man from Boston who was very well connected. If there was even a hint of mental illness…"

Donovan took a deep breath and continued. "I spent two weeks there, with Sarah. We told everyone, even Norah, that it was a vacation, long overdue."

"Norah believed you?"

"If she didn't, she kept her doubts to herself."

"Have you ever told her where you actually went?"

The old man shook his head. "After a while, I began to think I had made it up. I stopped drinking, cleaned up, put my life back together. When we came down from the mountains, I thought I had it out of my system. I couldn't wait to get back in a boat again. But when I got on board, I – I had to fight to keep myself from panicking. Every roll, every pitch, every screech of a seagull, I'd start shaking and sweating. One time it got so bad my clients thought I was having a heart attack.

"Finally, my nerves couldn't take it anymore. Cabot offered me and Sarah this place and I took it. Sold the boat and everything, and moved up here. After a while, I convinced myself that it *was* the booze and my imagination. But I was still afraid, and hiding here was easier than facing it, so I hid here. Then Sarah died and I... I began to remember the sea."

He sighed heavily and looked out over the still waters. "When Jensen asked me to pilot his boat upstream, it was like a holiday, Christmas and Easter in one. I couldn't wait to get on board and yet, I worried too, that the old nerves would give out on me. And they tried – I was jumpy as a cat on that deck. But I was fine – I made myself fine. I told myself that the feeling I had, about being fol-lowed, was just that – a feeling. Nothing more.

"I believed it, too. Until Jensen's boat got clawed up. Until that night when…"

He shuddered and snapped out of his reverie to look up at Emery. "I haven't told that story in years." He took a deep breath and laughed a little. "Sounds worse when you say it out loud, don't you think?"

When Emery didn't answer, Donovan turned to the water. "It's all right, Charles. I know you're probably going to agree with the townspeople." Though he tried to speak lightly, there was a tell-tale quiver in his tone. "Monsters aren't real and everyone knows that. But I know you'll do me the favor of *really* looking at this. I don't care what the truth is, so long as it *is* the truth. I need the truth, even if I'm too far crazy to believe it."

"I'll give you only the truth," Emery said. "That's a promise."

Even in the dark, Donovan's relief was plain.

"Thank you, Charles," he said.

As though on cue, Norah's voice echoed through the dark, calling them in for dinner.

7

As it turned out, Norah Donovan was an excellent cook and she knew how to feed hungry men. There were tiny boiled potatoes tossed in butter and onions, juicy pork chops, a tossed salad, and tapioca pudding for dessert. Emery, who hadn't really eaten since he'd rushed breakfast that morning (he didn't count the three bites he'd had of the hamburger or the cheese and crackers earlier that day), polished off two helpings. Donovan ate almost as much, causing Norah to say, "Why, Father! I haven't seen you eat like that in a long time."

"Pork chops are my favorite," he said merrily. "Also, it's been rather a long day."

He seemed like a man freed of his burden,

which made Emery wonder just how long he'd been carrying that load of memory by himself.

Probably since Sarah died, he thought.

Since Norah was watching him like a hawk ready to pounce, Emery kept the conversation light. He asked about the cottage and learned that Paul Cabot, despite being a policeman, had done very well during prohibition. This cottage was intended as a vacation rental, but he'd offered it to his sister and Donovan at a generous discount. Donovan was still grateful to Cabot, who'd passed away himself a few years ago.

"I would have wasted away if I wasn't able to get on the water somehow," he said through a mouthful of greens. "Even lake water will do in a pinch."

As such, it hadn't taken Donovan long to grow accustomed to lake sailing ("Boring compared to the Atlantic.") and he took great pride in his prowess at freshwater fishing. His neighbor, Jensen, and he had a long standing friendly rivalry that Donovan was currently winning, until his set back.

Hastily, lest Donovan slip back into reminisces,

Emery asked, "So how long have you been out here?"

"Ten years," Donovan said. "Norah was living in Boston then, working as chemist. Then two years ago, Sarah..." He cleared his throat. "Sarah became ill."

"I moved up to help my father with her care," Norah volunteered. "I've been here ever since."

Emery nodded thoughtfully. He knew Sarah had died a year ago, and yet here Norah remained. *Why?*

"She's the best nurse in the county," Donovan boasted. "Doc Whitcher wouldn't know what to do without her at the pharmacy."

That solved the mystery of how Norah was providing for herself in Deep Water, but not what happened to her mysterious beau with the old fashioned ideas about mental illness. Emery studied Norah when he could without her noticing. She was attentive to her father and took great pride in setting her table. Her antipathy towards Emery was a protective instinct more than an actual dislike. And she was a handsome woman, with large brown eyes, and, apparently, a strong work ethic and sense of pride. But there was no ring on her finger.

He was still musing on this when he realized that she was asking him a question.

"I'm sorry," he said. "Would you repeat that?"

"I asked if you were married," she said. She spoke in a tone so matter of fact that Emery felt as though someone had thrown cold water in his face.

"No, ma'am," he said, instinctively retreating back into his old manners. "I'm a confirmed bachelor. The Navy is not such a convenient career for raising a family."

"I tried to get him to quit and join me," Donovan said. "But Emery here is an old-fashioned kind of military man."

"All honor, no heart?" Norah asked in an innocent tone.

"Not everyone has the luxury of hearth and home, ma'am. Someone has to protect the homeland."

She had the grace to look uncomfortable. "Yes," she said thoughtfully. "I suppose you're right."

She rose and began to clear the table, nonverbally declaring the meal was over. Donovan went outside with Fido. Emery, despite Norah's protests, helped with the cleaning. They were just finishing when Donovan returned, still looking cheerful, but with a slight pallor in his face.

"I was going to listen to the radio a while," he said. "Care to join me, Charles?"

Emery declined and went outside to have a smoke and a think. He was standing by the lakeside, listening to the lapping of water and fingering the rosary in his pocket when he heard the back porch door open again.

He turned to see Norah quietly closing the door behind her. She'd thrown on a shawl around her shoulders and ran lightly over the patio and the grass to where he stood.

Emery was about to say something inane and polite – perhaps about the night being so nice – when she interrupted.

"Father hadn't told me he sent for you," she said, pulling the shawl tightly around herself, despite the fact that it wasn't cold. "I wasn't prepared."

"I'm sorry I put you out."

"I'm usually a better hostess," she admitted and looked out towards the lake.

There was a moment of silence. Emery offered her a cigarette, which she refused, and for some reason, this raised his opinion of her. He was tucking away the cigarette case, thinking what a pleasant night it really was, when she blurted out: "You think my father's crazy."

Emery let the statement hang there for a moment. He watched the smoke from his cigarette curl up into the night sky.

"Do you?" he asked finally.

"Of course not," she snapped.

"Then you believe in sea monsters?"

"No."

"Well then."

"He's *not* crazy," she said. "He's sick."

"Heart attacks do not cause delusions."

"So you're a doctor now?"

"I don't have to be."

She opened her mouth to reply, and then shut it again and glared.

"Yes, Miss Donovan," he said, in unsmiling sympathy. "That's my problem, too."

Emery took a drag on his cigarette and, when

her nose crinkled at the smoke, he flicked it to the side.

"He's…" Her voice was tremulous for a moment, until her anger returned and she steadied. "I lost my mother and my brother, Captain. I won't lose my father, not in this way."

"It's Chief," he corrected, kicking at the ground as he considered his next move. "Did your father ever tell you about the night Jasper Smith went overboard?"

"Yes…" When Emery looked at her, she shrugged. "It… may have been Mother who told me. I was away at school at the time. I only found out after. We don't talk about it much. Father took it very hard. Jasper was a close friend and he doesn't have many of those. Why do you ask?"

Emery didn't answer, just stood with his hands in his pockets, staring at his feet. He could almost hear the mechanisms whirling in Norah's head as she put two and two together.

"You don't mean…?" she whispered and the breeze seemed a little colder in her new-found fear. "That creature…? Oh no…"

"Did he ever tell you about the asylum he visited right after?"

"What nonsense are you talking about? He went to the mountains. For a rest, a vacation. He wasn't... He *isn't*..."

Her voice trailed off. She pressed a hand to her mouth.

"Why didn't he *tell* me?" she whispered.

"Maybe he didn't want his little girl losing faith in him."

She was very still. And then she took her hand from her mouth and said, "This can't get out. The psychologist we talked to said that... because there was no precedent, no history, I could... I could keep him home. Unless he turns dangerous. Which he *won't*. But if they find out about this – if they think he saw *this* back *then*..."

Her voice pitched upwards until it approached hysteria. Unconsciously, she stepped towards Emery, until she was only inches away, looking up at him, speaking in a curious blend of pleading and threat.

Emery looked down at her and winced in sympathy.

"I'm not telling anyone, Miss Donovan," he said quietly. "Not yet."

"Yet?"

"I promised your father I'd look into this matter. I promised a week. I won't say anything until that week is up. And only then if it's necessary." When Norah breathed a sigh of relief, he cautioned her: "I promised your father the truth, ma'am, and that's what he'll get."

She stepped back. "Monsters," she said bitterly. "What other conclusion can you come to?"

Despite her plain hostility towards him, Emery found himself wanting to leave her with a bit of comfort, something that she could hold on to, something that might soften her bitterness, even if only a little. So he said, "I'm thinking there might be a third option."

"What do you mean, a *third* option?"

"A third explanation that explains all of this. The boat *was* scarred, Miss Donovan, and something clawed up your father's arm and frightened him bad enough to induce a heart attack."

"But... what?"

"I don't know yet. But I can tell you this. I've

been around the world a few times and I've seen a lot of things. Good things, bad things, and worse things. Monsters exist, Miss Donovan. I've seen my fair share, but every single one of them was human." He looked down at his hands and said, "I can't promise you your father's sanity. That isn't up to me."

Now a small frown creased her brow. From somewhere in the distance, an owl hooted and Emery became aware of how dark it was and how tired he was. He turned towards the house. "I think its time I..." he started but she interrupted:

"I won't let you lock him up."

The cold certainty in her voice made him pause in his step. He turned to look at her again, a thin, sharp figure outlined against the moon's reflection on the water. Her long hair waved gently in the warm breeze, but the stiffness of her pose and the lift of her chin belied any softness.

"I won't let you call him crazy," she warned. "Whatever you find out, third option or no. He's my father. He's all I have. And I won't let him go."

For a moment, they stood there in starlight, a stand-off with no clear objective. Emery no more wanted her father to go to Whitcher Asylum than she did. Convincing her of that was a trick he didn't think he could accomplish tonight. Even so, if Donovan was crazy – and there was precious little to suggest that he was not – Emery had made a promise. He would be honest and he would do what had to be done. Donovan was counting on that. Emery wouldn't let him down.

Norah Donovan stood before him, her back to the lake, her arms folded, waiting on his reply.

After a moment, he nodded.

"We both have a promise to keep," he said. "Good night, Miss Donovan."

He left her standing by the water's edge, an un-smiling sentinel against the forces that threatened her world.

Part 2: The Third Option

Emery awoke at his usual time with a start. He found himself in a strange bed, staring at a strange ceiling. It was a moment before he remembered that he was in the guest room of Captain Donovan's lakeside house and further that he was here for one of two reasons: either to convince his old mentor that he was insane or prove the existence of a monster. Or the third option. None of these was appealing in the least.

He sat up, threw his legs over the side of the bed and stopped suddenly, groaning. His back was aching and his neck felt so stiff and sore that he had to gingerly knead it with his hands.

My own fault, he thought. *I shouldn't have fallen asleep outside.*

Last night, he'd bidden Norah goodnight and

went to his guest room. There, as quietly as possible, he dressed in jeans and a jacket, pocketing his utility knife and, after some hesitation, his small pistol too. He pulled out a small flashlight and waited in his room until the house quieted. Then he stole out of his room, down the stairs, and onto the back porch. The dog, Fido, had followed him, instinctively silent.

Outside, he'd grabbed a chair and sat on the end of the dock and waited. Fido, after sniffing around, settled at his feet and was soon asleep.

Emery waited for a long time, listening and watching. The partial moon played hide and seek with the clouds, sometimes shining its pure light on the gentle rippling waters, other times plunging him into near complete darkness. He listened, his ears straining, but there was little to hear. Across the waters, someone was playing their radio a touch too loudly. In the waters, there were the usual sounds of fish, jumping to catch insects. The dog's breathing and the creak of his own chair made for a comforting soundtrack.

He waited and he listened.

Despite his best efforts, somewhere between

the comfort of the night sounds, Norah's hearty meal, and his own exhaustion from a long drive, Emery fell asleep. He awoke with a start when a hand gently took his shoulder. He caught the scent of lavender before Norah's voice said, "What are you doing?"

He shook himself awake and looked at his watch, which he could just make out in the moonlight. It was nearly three in the morning.

"I was listening," he said, feeling a little foolish now. He turned to look at her, wincing at the crick in his neck.

She stood shivering on the dock, the wind whipping her unfashionably long hair across her face. One hand was holding her robe closed tightly over her sensible pajamas while the other shielded her eyes as she scanned his face.

"Listening for what?" she asked.

"It," he said.

She sighed. "I think you'll be more comfortable inside."

He had glanced at Fido, but the dog showed no uncommon interest in the lake or anything else. After a moment, Emery followed her back into the house. He had fallen asleep the instant his head hit the pillow.

His time in the port city had been enough for him to adjust to the steadiness of life on the shore, though he still hadn't quite acclimated to the silence of the country. But as he stirred, throwing off the blankets and stretching his back, he realized that it wasn't entirely silent. Someone was moving downstairs, making muffled sounds. Early morning birds chirped among the rustling of many leaves and the creaking sound of swaying pine trees. He'd left his window open a crack last night and a cool breeze stirred the still air in his room. It was peaceful, he had to admit. A different kind of peace than one found on the water, but peace nonetheless.

Emery got up and went out onto the landing. He caught sight of a flurry of silky robes rushing through the back porch door. He went halfway down the stairs and saw, through the doors, Norah's robed figure striding through the early-morning half-light with a towel over one shoulder and Fido frolicking at her side. She was heading for the docks and an early morning swim.

He took his kit to the bathroom, which was a tiny, cramped place obviously installed with summer living simplicity in mind. He managed to bathe in the small tub and heard the door shut on Norah's return, though he wasn't aware that he was listening for her. He was half-way through shaving when the boom of another door closing made him glance outside. Donovan ambled across the driveway, the new sun shining on his balding head. He was leaning less heavily on his cane today. He carried a rifle and whistled as he walked. Fido bounded at his side, clearly excited to be on the way to some adventure. They turned down a footpath that went into the woods behind the shed.

Emery was about to turn to the mirror again when an automobile pulled into the drive. The car was several years old, but clearly well-cared for. Its tomato red paint glittered in the sun. It was full of people, but it stopped at the end of the driveway, far enough away that Emery couldn't make out who the occupants were, just their outlines in the window.

Someone tooted a cheerful horn. A blond woman sprang out from the back door, laughing and swatting at the hand that attempted to pull her back in. She looked towards the house and her sweeping gaze settled on Emery's car. She pointed to it and approached it, looking up at the house with unconcealed curiosity. Emery was glad that light curtains shielded him from the blonde's gaze.

The downstairs door shut heavily and Norah stepped into Emery's view. She was dressed in a blue flowered dress and sturdy heels, her glistening towel-dried hair neatly combed and tucked up under a pale blue hat. The blond woman pointed to the car and Norah gestured towards the house. The blonde squinted upwards, trying to find him. Norah turned too and her gaze found Emery's.

She was a picture in that blue dress – feminine and graceful and pretty and Emery found himself wondering, once again, why she buried herself here, in this remote and forgotten place.

Norah's dress and the modest clothing of the blond woman reminded Emery that it was Sunday and he hadn't been to a service since his last day on sea. Too late to do anything about it now.

Emery lifted his razor in a greeting and Norah nodded. Then she turned and said something to the blonde woman. The blonde responded with a raised eyebrow and a saucy grin that earned her a friendly slap on the arm. Following Norah to the car, she kept glancing back curiously at Emery. Norah, however, entered the car without a backwards glance to the house. The car drove off, leaving a cloud of dust behind it.

When Emery had dressed, he came downstairs to the kitchen to find a table with a simple breakfast set up on it. There was a note by the coffee pot, written in a large hand:

Chief,

My father has a standing appointment with Mr. Jensen next door to go hunting every Sunday. I encouraged him to keep it. He'll be gone all day, if the weather holds. I've gone to church and will be back in a few hours.

Norah

He looked down at the table, which was set for one with bread, jam, butter, and hard-boiled eggs in a cup.

She doesn't like that I'm here, but she's still

the consummate hostess, he thought and shook his head. *Will I ever understand women?*

He didn't think that was likely, so he dismissed the possibility. When he was done eating, he poured himself another cup of the cooling coffee and wandered over to the back door. Stepping outside, he breathed in the fresh morning air and closed his eyes to soak in the warmth of the sun. The sound of the shallow lapping water filled him with a yearning to go out. When he opened his eyes again, Deep Water Lake glittered like diamonds, but the first thing he saw was the island.

"The official explanation is that my father was attacked by someone living on the island who wanted his boat."

"Did anyone search the island?"

"All we found were the remains of a campfire..."

Donovan's hopeful, "Where do we start?" rang through Emery's head and he answered into the empty air, "We start on the island."

9

There was a small, recently painted rowboat tied up at the end of Donovan's dock. Emery hopped in and immediately checked all around the sides, but there were no scarring. Whatever or whomever had damaged the *Daisy Jane* had ignored this vessel.

He loosened the lines, pushed away from the dock, and bent his back to the oars. Early though it was during the day, the sun warmed his back and the stillness in the air warned of humidity ahead. A few insects sung, but otherwise, the lake was silent – the partiers of last night were probably still sleeping off their hangovers. Emery had the water to himself, and he relished in the privacy. The roll beneath him was comfortingly familiar and his muscles warmed to the familiar exercise – pull, push, pull, push. It wasn't long at all before he was in the shadows of the narrow island.

Last night Emery had learned, from the map on Donovan's living room wall, that this long, narrow island was called Loon Island. It was thin and heavily forested, and too rocky and narrow for any building. It was close enough to Donovan's side of the lake that a healthy, fit man (or woman) could swim out and back without a problem.

Emery kept this in mind when he pulled himself on to the rocky shore. His craft bumped up against the granite that jutted up from the water and the moment his feet touched the pine-strewn ground, small insects came out to investigate.

He swatted them away and stepped into the cool shade of the trees. The terrain was typical of New England – rocky and uneven, with tall pines overhead and short ferns and wild blueberry bushes underfoot. A few birds chirped overhead. When he moved, the insects weren't quite so bad. Once, when he placed his hand on a tree trunk, he was startled by a tree frog, staring at him with an almost Buddhist calm.

He worked his way through the island until he

came to the point off of which Donovan was fishing that fateful night. Here, the island narrowed even more and terminated in an open, sandy point. The opposite shore was further away than Donovan's side and it was heavily wooded with few houses. Emery could only make out four houses amid the shifting, bobbing landscape of trees and branches. Norah had mentioned that these vacation cottages were empty most of the year.

Emery stepped out onto the point and looked around. The map indicated that the lake was deep here, with a slight current. It was silent, too – as quiet as you could get out here in the middle of the woods. In the distance, he heard a muffled crack of gunfire, then a second shot. It might have been Donovan and Jensen, but Emery was struck by how natural the sound was – it seemed a part of the musical suite of forest noises.

You're becoming poetical in your old age.

He studied the water. Ripples wrinkled the surface. A few insects danced tentatively close to the water and as he watched, there was a flash of fin and scale and open mouth. The surviving insects scattered and Emery thought, *Hunters lay both above and beneath this lake.*

Emery turned inward and stepped through the undergrowth and the fallen branches until he came across the campsite.

There were signs of disturbance among the pine-strewn ground. Heavy boots, probably the sheriff's, had churned up the ground and were over-lain with smaller boot marks, presumably Norah's. Some of the disturbances had been smoothed over again, as though someone had sat where Norah and the sheriff had scuffed up.

The remnants of a lean-to sagged against a low and bare tree limb. The fire itself had been carefully built and tended. Someone had gone to the trouble of digging out the ground and lining a small pit with rocks. The absence of matchsticks made Emery think the person had flint, but matchsticks could have been burnt as well.

He looked around. The campsite was nestled in the densest part of the island, invisible to anyone looking from the shore.

It must have been the old man's screams that

drove this stranger out to look, Emery mused. *But why hide here? Why not steal the boat?*

There was a small pile of ashes in the fire pit and he bent to examine them and touched them lightly. They were flaky and untouched by the rain yesterday morning. Someone had been here, more recently than the sheriff's investigation last week. They'd relit the fire and sat near it to warm themselves. It was either a bold move or a desperate one.

And they might still be here.

Emery looked up and around. Instinctively, his hand went under his jacket, where his pistol was. But nothing moved in the woods, save the breeze stirring the trees and he heard nothing but the whispers of leaves overhead and the soft lapping of water against rock.

Nevertheless, he did a complete survey of the tiny island, walking around it until he found a spot on the sandy side, the shore facing away from Donovan's shore, where the water hadn't yet washed away the signs of foot prints and the mark of a small raft, touching ground.

He examined what little remained of the foot prints – bare feet, either a small man or a woman's steps. He saw both heel and toe, which indicated that the party hadn't run. He walked around the rest of the island, but found no indication that the person had returned.

He returned to the campsite. He examined the ground in and around the lean-to, but there was little to be seen there. Someone had lain beneath the lean-to, but Emery was not skilled enough to detect how long they'd been there. Running his hands through the leaves and pines turned up nothing to indicate what the culprit had been eating or drinking. The islander, whomever he or she was, was very careful indeed.

Emery returned to the point where Donovan reported his encounter and stood there for a moment, thinking. His gaze slipped down into the water and froze.

Then, swiftly, he tore off his jacket, rolled up his sleeve, and stepped into the water, wetting his shoes. He plunged his arm into the freezing lake, up to his elbow and then deeper still, until his rolled shirt sleeve was soaking. He felt around, his hand sliding over slippery rocks and rough twigs, nearly slipping as he crouched and reached. But eventually, his hand found what he was searching for and he came up in triumph, clutching the tool that he'd seen through the water's surface. It was an ice pick, with a wooden handle and a sharp blade. And judging from the wood of the handle, it had not been in the water longer than a week.

10

As promised, Norah returned from her outing at about noon. Emery had changed out of his wet clothes, and was now working in the side yard near the driveway. The same shiny red car appeared with its laughing crowd and discharged her from its interior with a cheerful toot of the horn and many hands waving from windows and doorways.

"See you next week!" the blonde called. She caught sight of Emery, standing behind the *Daisy Jane* with the ice pick in one hand and a rag in the other, and waved cheerfully.

Norah, still smiling, turned to see who the blonde was waving at and Emery was struck by her expression. With the bright noon sun shining on her hair until it looked like polished mahogany, she was enchanting.

Like any enchantment, it was over too soon. She sobered on seeing him and her relaxed manner evaporated like the mist. The happy chariot drove off, taking its merry laughter with it and she began to stroll over to him, tucking her scarf into her bag. Her eyes looked worried again and Emery had to remind himself that he was one of the physical reminders that all was not well in her world.

Nevertheless, the sharp change of attitude annoyed him and he bent back to his work.

"Good morning, Miss Donovan," he said.

"Good morning." She sounded uncertain that it *was* a good morning. "Did you sleep all right?"

She was close now and in another second would be able to see that he wasn't doing very much at all – his conclusions had already been drawn. So he straightened back up, rubbing his hands on the rag, and nodding.

"Yes, thank you," he said. "Thank you for breakfast. It was nice to have a cup of good coffee in the morning."

He moved over to the woodpile and she

followed. On the ground near the pile, he'd lain out a variety of boards, the remnants of an old crate. Her eyes widened when she saw how they were scarred and scored.

"What are you doing?" she asked.

"I'm trying to figure out exactly what made the scratches on your father's boat." He gestured to the *Daisy Jane* with the ugly crisscross of scarring on her keel. "Look, see the placement? The spacing between the cuts? And look at the scuffing around the railing here."

She stepped in close and bent to see where he pointed out. "So?"

"So I tried to duplicate them." He stepped around her and pointed to the first board. "That I did with your father's fillet knife. The gouges are too narrow to correspond with the ones on your father's boat. So I tried my pocket knife, a regular kitchen knife, a shell..."

"A *shell*?" she repeated in disbelief, but he went right on. "

"I also used rocks, a fork, and this." He pulled out the ice pick and handed it to her. "I found that in the waters where your father claimed he was attacked."

"An ice pick?"

"It could have been tossed from one of those party boats, but it was awfully close to the island's shore."

"The hobo," she said, holding the ice pick as though it might slip and cut her. "So you think he did this."

He leaned on the keel and looked at her. "Why?"

"Why... what?"

"Why would a vagrant try to carve up Jensen's boat and then your father's?"

"Maybe he wanted to steal it." She stopped and frowned. "But then..."

"Why would he return the boat to your dock with your father still in it?" Emery finished for her and nodded. "Exactly."

She frowned, tapping the ice pick against her other hand. "Things have been going missing around here lately. We lost some stuff from our clothesline just the other day."

"What did you lose?"

"Nothing much. One of my father's old sweaters and a pair of his socks."

"So our vagrant is a man."

"Aren't they usually?"

He grinned. "There are always exceptions. In any case, we are left with the same problem: Why would a vagrant go through all the trouble of frightening your father into a heart attack and unconsciousness, only to leave the boat with the owner?"

She sighed and handed the ice pick back. "You're right, that doesn't make sense."

He took the ice pick and, seeing her crestfallen expression, grinned again. "Don't look so dejected. We tested a theory and it didn't work. That's progress. It's one less theory to think about." He bent to collect up the tools he'd left scattered on the ground.

Norah shrugged and turned toward the lake. "I guess... I had more hope pinned on that third option you were talking about."

He looked up then. She had her back to him and was rubbing her arm in a distracted way.

Something in her posture, her voice, told him that she was fighting back tears.

"I still believe there's a third explanation, Norah." She turned back to him and he went on, "I'm stubborn. It'll take more than one bad theory to make me give up on this."

The small smile that split her face was like the sun breaking through the clouds. The moment held – and then, as though conscious that she was saying more than she meant, Norah broke eye contact with him and stepped back toward the boards on the ground.

"You didn't say which board was the closest to the scarring," she said.

Emery found his voice and just barely got out, "It was…" when the roar of a large engine cut through the peace of the morning.

A flashy car, black and gleaming and new, roared into the driveway, kicking up dust. It jerked to a halt beside Emery's borrowed auto and settled like a beast. The back passenger door was flung open and a man in a natty suit hopped out.

"Norah, my darling, I have returned to you!" he exclaimed, pulling off his hat exuberantly.

Norah stiffened. "Philip!"

The man, Philip, waved jauntily, and then turned to pull a suitcase out of the car. Through the windows, Emery could see two other men inside, neither smiling and both definitely of a different class than Philip. The driver was in a dark, well-cut suit and even from this distance, Emery could see that his hair was carefully trimmed and well oiled. His face was all angles and shadows. He flipped the remains of a cigarette out of the window, eyeing Emery like he might be trouble. The passenger was more difficult to see – he was smoking a cigar and seemed unmoved by anything that was going on. There was a heaviness to these two men – like they were on a mission and nothing, not even social niceties, would stop them.

Philip, by contrast, looked for all the world like a snake oil salesman. He was stocky, but trim, with short dark hair and a long face that might have been handsome had he not been so cocky. His clothes were expensive, as were his shoes, but his suitcase was a shoddy, beaten affair that had never been worth much. When he turned back to Norah, his smug arrogant smile and falsetto bonhomie was enough to put Emery on the alert.

All of this Emery saw in the space of the few seconds that it took Philip to pull his suitcase out of the car. As soon as the door swung shut, the driver shoved the car into reverse. The engine roared as the driver swung into a quick two-point turn and shot off down the road, leaving Philip coughing in the kicked-up dust.

He waved his hand to clear the air as he strode over to where Norah stood, rigid and unwelcoming. His dark eyes took in her and Emery, and his smile deepened unpleasantly.

"Have I come at a bad time?" he asked in false innocence.

Norah didn't even try to hide her distaste. "Philip, what are you doing here?"

His eyes widened in feigned hurt. "Why, my dear sweet, homebody cousin, Uncle Harry told me I was welcome anytime!"

"Uncle?" Emery said. "Cousin?"

Norah started as though she'd just remembered that he was there. "This is my cousin, Philip

Cabot. Philip, Chief Petty Officer Charles Emery. A friend of my father's."

"Oh, he's your *father's* friend," Philip said with a laugh. His hand, when Emery shook it, was weak and cold as a fish. "Chief Petty Officer – that sounds important. Are you here for the fishing, Chief Petty Officer?"

"Yes," Emery lied, annoyed. "You can call me Emery."

"Fine, fine," Philip said. He placed his suitcase on the ground and stood with his feet spread wide, as though asserting ownership of the ground. "How long are you staying?"

"About a week."

"That's a good length for a vacation. And are you staying around here, Emery?"

"Not around," Norah said. "Here."

Philip's eyebrows shot up. "Oh," he purred. "Really? I suppose she gave you the blue bedroom? The favored guest *always* gets the blue bedroom, which I suppose leaves me the green one. Unless you have any other of *your father's* friends staying with you this weekend, Norah, darling."

Emery wanted to hit him.

Norah said wearily: "No, Philip. Mr. Emery is our only guest."

"Splendid!" Philip picked up his suitcase and beamed at the pair of them. "Then this will be a relaxing week. I hope you're a poker player, Chief. Uncle Harry and I are at the card table every night whenever I'm in town."

"Who are your friends?" Norah asked.

"Oh, them?" Philip shrugged with exaggerated innocence. "Just some men who offered me a ride."

"A ride in your own car?"

This startled Emery and the question caused the arrogant Cabot to wince.

"Why do they have *your* car, Philip?" she insisted. "What happened?"

Philip smiled and shrugged. "The stakes were unusually high last night," he said smoothly.

"Oh, Philip!"

"Not to worry, not to worry. I always have a backup plan. And a big part of that plan is to spend time with you and Uncle Harry in the splendid isolation of nature, away from temptation in all its forms." He smiled at them. "But here I've interrupted your.... conversation? With Uncle Harry's old chum? Don't mind me, dear, I'll head into the house and unpack. No need to accompany me, I know the way!"

He started toward the house, then turned, walking backwards as he called, "I'll be in for dinner, naturally, Norah, but don't make anything fancy on my account."

Emery hadn't realized how tightly he was clenching his jaw until the man was on the porch. He turned and saw Norah, still standing rigidly with her hands balled into fists, her expression bordering on fear.

"Do you want me to get rid of him?" he asked. When she looked at him, startled, Emery explained, "I can drive him into town, insist he stay there. You don't have to let him walk all over you."

She laughed, bitter and short: "That's just it," she said. "I do."

Emery digested this for a moment, then he put the tools down on top of the overturned boat.

"Come on," he said. "I'm taking you into town for lunch."

orah was too relieved to reject Emery's invitation. Once the car was on the road, she lowered her window and the resulting noise from the wind was enough to keep the conversation from starting. Emery let her have her silence. Philip Cabot's arrival had upset her. Emery could very well chalk this up to an unwillingness to have an obviously unsympathetic local on hand in the middle of a private crisis, but he didn't think that this was the whole explanation. Glancing at his passenger, he saw concern etched deeply into her face.

Cabot...

Within twenty minutes, they were in a booth at the local diner, the same one that Emery had stopped in on his way into town. Minnie was serving again and gave them a look of unfeigned curiosity. From the way Norah's shoulders stiffened, Emery could see that, though she expected to be an object of attention, she hadn't quite grown accustomed to it.

They placed their orders for sandwiches and coffee and as the waitress strode away, Emery remarked, "I seem to be causing all sorts of speculation today."

Norah looked surprised, then she shook her head.

"It isn't just you," she said, tucking a loose strand of hair behind her ear. "I've only been in town less than two years – I'm not a local yet. Neither is Dad, come to think of it, and he's been here ten."

"How long does it take to become a local?"

"You have to be born here. Or marry one, I think. Florence Jensen is from Watertown, Connecticut, but she's considered one of them now. Of course, she married Mr. Jensen about twenty five years ago. I'll have to ask her how long it took to stop being the new girl."

"So you intend to stay? For a while, I mean?"

Again, she appeared surprised by the question.

"I hadn't thought about it, really," she said. "I came because of Dad. I guess I'll stay until he doesn't need me anymore."

Their conversation was interrupted by Minnie, who brought them two mugs and poured them steaming coffee from a well-worn pot. She brought cream at Norah's request. Emery waited to speak until after Minnie was behind the counter again, tending to another customer. Then he leaned forward and lowered his voce.

"Miss Donovan," he said. "You had no idea about the previous encounter with the creature?"

She had been stirring her coffee, lost in thought. Now she looked at him with worried eyes.

"No," she said quietly.

"But you weren't surprised to hear it."

"No. He was too willing to believe it, you know? He should have thought it was something else – an animal or a person or the drink. Something. But he stuck with the monster." She shrugged. "At least until last Monday."

"What happened last Monday?"

She kept her eyes on her coffee. "I don't know. My father wouldn't tell me. I came home and he'd been drinking, heavily. I knew other men had been there, because of the drinking glasses, but he wouldn't tell me who had come or why. All he did was write a letter and asked me to post it." She looked at him. "It must have been your letter."

"Probably. He stopped talking about the monster then?"

"He nearly stopped talking altogether. Finally, when I threatened to go to the sheriff and report that he'd been intimidated, he told me not to worry, he'd sort things out. Then you came."

Behind Norah, the door swung open and Tom Murphy and Joe Barker stepped in, talking. Barker was in a bright mood, but Murphy was his usual taciturn self. He spotted Emery first, then Norah and took a half step in their direction but Minnie called his attention to the two cups of coffee she had ready on the counter and he turned toward her.

Norah continued, unaware, "My father – he's a fisherman. He tells stories. But he's never been unable to separate facts from reality. Until now."

Minnie appeared with their sandwiches. Emery waited until she went back to the counter. Murphy and Barker were in quiet conversation. Covert glances in their direction warned him of their topic of discussion.

He ignored them and took a bite. Norah picked up her sandwich, eyed it, and then put it down again.

"What happened, Emery? That last time, with Jasper?"

Emery swallowed, and then gave her a quick rundown of Donovan's previous encounter with the creature. He omitted the finer details and left her to draw her own conclusions. She listened without interruption and without touching her food. When he mentioned the asylum, she drew in a sharp breath, as if in pain.

"An asylum!" she whispered. Her face was pale, as though she'd been slapped. "I was hoping you'd made that up."

"It was a brief visit," Emery said. "He got a clean bill of health."

"It's history," she said, leaning forward, her face hard. Her finger beat on the table to emphasize her point. "It's precedent. If this gets out..."

Emery glanced at the counter. Murphy, Barker, and Minnie all turned away at his gaze.

"Miss Donovan, we are being observed," he said.

She looked over at the counter and saw, for the first time, Murphy and Barker. Her jaw set and she drew a steadying breath. She leaned back into her booth and nodded.

"Sorry," she said.

Emery gestured to the bar. "When I arrived here, the sheriff was talking to those men. He seemed to think that they intimidated your father. Do you think that's likely?"

"Tom Murphy, yes. Joe Barker…" she shrugged. "It wouldn't have been his idea, but he would have gone along to see the action."

"Are they violent?"

Her brown eyes clouded. "I don't know. They drink. But I don't know." She hesitated, and then leaned forward. "I want to be clear about something, Mr. Emery," she said. "About my father and… his problem. I don't care about our reputation or the… stigma surrounding something like this. My mother would have cared, but I don't care about what people think of me personally. I'm not afraid of being alone. What I do care about is my father. If he's locked up, he'll... It can't happened, Mr. Emery. I can't allow it."

"Do you really think we can stop it?"

"If I can, I will," she said and paused before continuing. "While my father was in the hospital, the sheriff came to us. He wanted Father to be evaluated, but Father refused, of course, and I didn't press it for obvious reasons. I went by myself, without telling either one of them. I explained what happened and explained that I wanted to keep my father at home with me. The doctor told me that as long as there wasn't a history – which I thought there wasn't at the time – and as long as Father wasn't violent, I could.

"What I didn't realize was, after my father refused, that Sheriff Young also went to see the psychologist and got the same story. Young came to my work and told me that if there was even a hint of violence, he wouldn't hesitate to lock my father up. So I told *him* that I wasn't afraid, that there was no past history and no violence and therefore this matter was at an end."

She stopped and swallowed hard. "But what

you're telling me now is, there was a past history and Father is…"

Emery interrupted. "Nothing has changed, Miss Donovan," he said firmly. "Nothing."

"If Sheriff Young finds out about Portsmouth, he'll take my father away. He told me that."

"If Sheriff Young finds out, it won't be from you or me." He paused. "But could he find out from someone else?"

"That first doctor, you mean?"

"Those records would be confidential. I meant someone closer to home."

She frowned, and then her eyes went wide. "You mean Philip? But… he wouldn't know. Would he?"

"Your uncle, Paul Cabot, was the police officer your father called to report the first incident. It was he that suggested the sanitarium and he that covered everything up."

"Uncle Paul?" She shook her head. "Actually, that sounds like him. He was always mixed up in things. My mother always thought he had something on the side during prohibition."

"He wouldn't have been the only one. But

would he have told anyone about your father and the asylum?"

"No." She was firm on that point. "He loved my mother, and the scandal, the disgrace would have killed her. He'd have done anything for her, or me."

"His wife, maybe?"

"I doubt it. We always got the impression she knew less about his dealings than anyone else. She passed away a year after him, so there's no asking her now."

"How about their children?"

"There was only Philip and he was at college then. Philip never could keep a secret, even when we were kids, so I doubt..."

She went silent for a moment, so coldly still that Emery knew something had occurred to her.

"What is it?"

"Philip," she said and looked at him, thought-fully. "He... He *was* upset about the terms of Uncle Paul's will."

"About your uncle leaving your father the house, you mean?"

"Well, that just it. He didn't leave it to Father.

Not exactly." She leaned forward again. "Uncle Paul made a lot of money, especially during the twenties. When he died, he left everything to Philip, but his will stipulated that my father was allowed the use of the lake house for as long as he wanted it. Philip can't touch the house until my father either dies or leaves it."

Emery nodded slowly, taking that in. "I'm guessing that Philip didn't like that?"

"I don't think Philip really cared at first. It isn't worth much, especially now since the crash, and Philip had so many other assets that I don't think he gave it much thought. But now..."

"He gambles," Emery said.

Norah nodded. "And loses. A lot."

Emery nodded thoughtfully and leaned forward. "So maybe..."

He was interrupted by the door swinging open again, this time with more force. A man strode into the room, tall and broad shouldered and carrying himself like he owned the place, though it was clear from Minnie's expression that she'd never seen him before. His suit was expensive and exquisitely cut and his hat was tipped at a sharp angle. The bill he held was crisp and new. Emery recognized him even before the man looked around the nearly-empty restaurant. It was the man who'd driven off in Philip's car.

"Got change for a dollar, doll?" he asked Minnie.

Minnie, looking both terrified and intrigued, nodded and leaned forward over the counter to take it from his hand. "Coming right up. Would you like coffee with that?"

"Just the cash, doll, just the cash."

Barker, ever willing to cause trouble, leaned forward. "Here for the fishing, mister?" he asked. "Or the monster?

The newcomer looked at him and his lip curled into a sardonic smile.

"Sure," he said and laughed. "I came to bag me a monster! I figure it'd look good on my wall, you know what I mean?"

Tom Murphy's face turned pale. The look he shot at Norah said, *this is* your *fault.*

Minnie smiled at the stranger. "Here's your change," she said and dumped the coins into his tanned hand. "Come back any time."

"Thanks, doll. When I bag me a monster, I'll

save you a claw," the man drawled and pocketed the lot. He gave Barker another look and laughed, "Fishing!" before he sauntered out again.

Emery and Norah watched through the window as he walked over to the gas station, where the other man, his passenger, stood, smoking and watching the attendant top off the water. Across the street, leaning in the doorway of a closed mercantile, Sheriff Young was also watching, his broad face void of any expression.

"That's Philip's car," Norah said. She looked at Emery. "Philip was up here the week before last and he'd lost then, too. He always comes to the lake house to recuperate after he loses and last week was a big one. I've never seen him so nervous, so upset. He asked both me and Father for money, but of course, we didn't have anything more than a few bucks between us. He has some assets left, I think, but nothing liquid."

"So he was around when the incident occurred?"

"No. He'd left that morning. He said he'd found a way out of his debts."

"How?"

"I assumed he'd found someone to lend him money. I made him promise that he'd stop gambling and get back to work, but his promises are worth less than the air he uses to make them."

Outside, the city man emerged from the gas station, call complete, putting his hat on. The other pulled himself up from his slouching position and tossed a coin at the attendant. He threw his hat into the back seat as he climbed into Philip's car. Emery watched, wondering what it must have cost Norah's cousin to turn the keys for such a handsome vehicle over to a virtual stranger.

Norah said. "He lost the car. I can't believe he lost the car."

"He seemed pretty certain he was going to get it back."

The engine roared as the two men in the shiny car disappeared around the bend. Sheriff Young watched them go before crossing the street to where the poor gas station attendant was waiting for the next interrogation.

Emery saw Norah's expression change from shock to consideration. He'd expected a half-hearted attempt to defend her wayward cousin. He thought it very telling when instead, she nodded, slow and thoughtful.

"He did say he had a backup plan," she said softly and her eyes hardened. "Maybe…"

"Yes." Emery looked at her. "Maybe we found our third explanation."

When Emery insisted that they go to Sheriff Young, Norah was horrified.

"We don't know anything yet," she protested. "All we have is a theory."

"Did you report the theft of the shirt and socks?"

"I wouldn't waste his time. Besides, things are hard enough for those people without being thrown in jail for stealing socks. I'm no Inspector Javert."

"I think we should report it."

"Whatever for?"

"If we're right about your cousin," Emery said, "then it's likely that he hired someone to scare your uncle back into the asylum. That vagrant is the only person we know who was on the spot. And even if he *wasn't* hired by your cousin, he's still the only witness we know of."

Norah looked thoughtful.

"I hadn't thought about that," she admitted and flushed when Emery gave her a critical look. "I was too busy trying *not* to think about worse things."

He grinned. "I can understand that." He started to rise from the booth and stopped when Norah reached out and grasped his sleeve.

"Charles," she said. It was the first time she'd used his first name and Emery was surprised at how nice it sounded. "Do we have to bring Philip into this with the sheriff?"

Emery lowered himself back into the seat. "I guess we don't."

"Then don't. He's still family and if we're wrong..."

"You don't think Young will put the pieces together?"

She shrugged. "If he does, he does. But I don't want the shame of turning an innocent man in to the police if I can help it. Can we avoid it?"

"If I can, I will."

She reluctantly went along.

Sheriff Young didn't seem particularly impressed when they appeared in his office. He was still less so with the story they posited to him. After briefly introducing them to his lanky deputy, Boone, he leaned back in his office chair, threw his feet up onto the desk and listened without looking at them, tossing a coin up and catching it.

Emery calmly told the sheriff about his prowl around the island and his discovery of the ice pick. Young's eyes glinted when Emery produced it and he grunted, "You've got good eyes, Captain."

"I'm a seaman. I'm used to looking through the water. And it's Chief."

The sheriff nodded and examined the ice pick carefully. The tip was worn and had been worn since before Emery had tried using it himself. "You think this hobo attacked Captain Donovan?"

"I'm sure the thought has occurred to you."

He put the ice pick on the desk. "It had, but then, who would try to scare a man to death, then save his life?"

"Someone who was trying to frighten him,"

Norah supplied. "Someone who was trying to call his sanity into question."

Sheriff Young looked at her warily. "Is that what you think this is about, Miss Donovan?"

"What else could it be? Monsters?"

"You know what I think it is." He turned his attention back to the ice pick. "That looks about the right size for the scarring."

"That's what I thought," Emery said. "Of course, I haven't compared it to the Jensen's boat yet."

"You won't be able to. It's in the shop, already repaired." He tapped his desk and then looked at Emery. "Where was this?"

"In the shallows by the point of the island. Near where the Captain's incident occurred."

"So this was within throwing distance of the Captain's boat?"

Norah erupted before Emery could speak. "You think my *father* did this?" Her eyes flashed with anger. "You think he damaged his own boat?"

"I'm just sorting through the possibilities."

"That's *not* a possibility. That's just malicious!"

"Miss Donovan." Sheriff Young's tone was low

and warning. "I'm going to have to ask you to calm down."

She slammed her palm into her chair rail, but she didn't say anything more. Emery, whose own patience was wearing thin, said wearily, "Sheriff, what reason would Captain Donovan have for attacking his own boat? This story about the monster has only hurt him, not helped and he has no grudge against the Jensens."

"Well, now," the sheriff said, coolly. "I guess I just like to consider all possibilities."

Emery frowned at Young. The sheriff was self-satisfied and bullish, and yet, for all that, there was something calculating behind his façade of the typical small-minded, small-town lawman. Emery could sense it, but he didn't trust it. That sort of mind could just as easily corrupt as help and he wasn't in the mood to deal with one more rotten apple.

Young interrupted his thoughts. "Just why *are* you here, Mr. Emery? Small town fishing can't possibly appeal to a man of your experience, now, can it?"

His tone was calculated to be offensive. Emery just smiled.

"Oh, I don't know," he said sweetly. "I rather like it around here." Then, before Young could press, he went on: "There was a robbery at the Donovan's. I convinced Miss Donovan here that she ought to report it."

"Robbery?" Young frowned and swung his feet down from the desk to turn on Norah. "What was taken? Why didn't you report this?"

"Because of what was taken," she said stiffly. "Someone swiped two pairs of black socks and my father's navy and yellow striped sweater from our clothes line the other day. I didn't think it was important, but Mr. Emery thought it was."

"Did he?" the sheriff turned back to Emery, cocking a lazy eyebrow. "And just why did you think this was so important, Chief Emery?"

"Because there was only one witness that we know of the night of Captain Donovan's attack," Emery said calmly. "And now we know what he's wearing."

***

Sheriff Young reluctantly took note of the missing items and promised that he and his men would keep an eye out for a stranger wearing a large navy and yellow sweater. He warned Norah that he'd be coming by to check on things.

"You're father had a shock," he said. "Seems the neighborly thing to do, to check on him."

Outside his office, Norah fumed.

"He's just like a sheriff out of one of those dime-store novels," she growled, pulling on her gloves. "Small-minded, suspicious, and a bully."

Emery didn't think it wise to concur or defend the sheriff. He was opening the passenger door for Norah when his eye caught a glimpse of Phillip's car, pulling in to a space in front of one of Deep Water's hotels. The two thugs, still smoking, got out of the car, heads swiveling as they checked out the street. One of them, the passenger, walked around to the trunk of the car and lifted the door. The other stepped up on to the porch and kept a casual watch on the street as his companion pulled out two small bags.

"What is it?" Norah asked, seeing Emery's

distraction. Her eyes widened when she caught sight of the two men.

"I guess your cousin was telling the truth," he said. "They are staying in town."

"But why?"

"That's what I was wondering."

Sheriff Young's voice boomed behind Emery, making him jump. He turned as the sheriff let the screen door swing shut and stepped out further on to the porch. Young shielded his eyes as he studied the two men in the distance.

"Friends of yours, Captain?" he asked Emery, in that same tone of casual malice.

"No, sheriff," Emery said, suddenly tired of the sly sheriff's suspicions. "And it's Chief."

"Came into town only a day after you, also driving a flashy car. Thought you might know them."

"It's a big world, sheriff, and I'm a sailor. I don't know everyone in a flashy car."

The two men slouched into the hotel and disappeared from sight. The sheriff dropped his arm.

"That car looks familiar," he said. "I've been trying to place it all morning." He fixed Emery with an amused, searching stare. "So, you've never seen those two men before?"

"I didn't say that." Emery shut Norah's door and walked around to his own side.

"Then you have seen them before."

"Yup." Emery opened his door and slid into the front seat.

The sheriff responded by placing his hand on the roof of the car and bending down low so he could look through Norah's open window. "Where, Chief?" he growled.

"At my house, Sheriff," Norah said. "They dropped Philip off this morning. They're friends of his. Ask him."

"I'll do that, ma'am," he said. "Might have known they were Phillip's friends. He doesn't keep with the best and brightest now, does he?"

"What my cousin does is his own business," Norah said stiffly. "Now, if you don't mind, we have things to do." She turned to Emery. "Can you stop by the pharmacy? I have a prescription to pick up."

Emery grinned. "Yes, ma'am," he said and, "Good afternoon, Sheriff!"

He drove off, leaving the sheriff to muse in the dust kicked up by their car.

"I thought you wanted to leave Philip out of this," Emery said.

"I did. But I think that's impossible, don't you?"

They were passing Philip's car, dust-coated and cooling in the shade of the false-fronted hotel. Emery glanced at it and nodded as he shifted.

"I do." After a moment, he said, "Do you really need something at the pharmacy?'

"Yes, why?"

"I had an idea. Are you up to taking a little trip with me?"

Norah stared at him, surprised. But she didn't say no.

13

The pharmacy was normally closed on Sunday, but Norah worked there during the week and had a key. While she was collecting her prescription – heart medication for her father - Emery used the pay phone in the corner. It took him a number of calls before he secured the information that he was looking for. When he stepped out of the little booth, Norah was waiting for him by the counter, fanning herself with a tourist brochure.

"Got what you need?" she asked.

"Yes, I did," he said, and waved his notebook triumphantly. "Doctor Otis Skinner."

"Skinner? Who is that?"

"He was the man that treated your father in that rest home ten years ago."

"Oh!" she looked nervous. "What did he say?"

"I haven't spoken to him yet. I talked to the head nurse at the rest home and she told me that he was gone with his wife for the weekend at their lake house. When I called his house, his wife said that he'd be glad to see me, but that he was out on the lake. He'd be back in time for dinner at 5, if we cared to see him before or during."

"What town?"

"Holloway."

"That's an hour's drive from here, in a reasonably fast car."

"Which, I have.' He gestured out the door. "Want to come?"

She sighed. "I'd be lying if I said yes. But I suppose I ought to."

"That," Emery said, "is not the most enthusiastic confirmation I've ever received from a woman. But in your case, I'll take it."

She grinned and preceded him out the door. "If all your invitations were so staid and proper, I'd be surprised they weren't less enthusiastic."

"Miss Donovan, you wound me."

"Oh, just drive, will you?"

***

The drive to Holloway was long and pretty... and quiet. Despite her teasing tone earlier, Norah lapsed into silence as the road stretched before them. After a short bout of asking questions, Emery let her sit and think. She was worried about her father and doubtless fearful of whatever Doctor Skinner was going to tell them... if he was going to tell them anything of use, that was.

Emery could understand her trepidation. She was the type of woman who would be resigned to the truth and should the doctor confirm that her father had suffered from madness, she would probably accept it - and continue to treat her father at home. If she *didn't* hear this from the doctor, she would likely keep ignoring the evidence and stubbornly insist on her father being nothing more than a man who liked to drink and spin tales. Some people preferred their ignorance to a painful truth, but Emery had always been a firm believer that if you faced reality head on, you were the better for it.

A half hour had gone by in silence before he attempted to talk again.

"Your father told me you came up from Boston to take care of your mother," he said.

She started, then nodded. "Yes, I worked in a hospital in Boston. In the labs, actually."

"Sounds like fascinating work."

"It was. I miss it sometimes."

"Why haven't you gone back?"

She shrugged. "My father needs me and he's not a city man." She looked at him curiously. "Are you married, Chief?"

He shook his head and kept his eyes on the road. "No, ma'am. You?"

"No."

"Hard to believe you were never asked."

"I didn't say that."

"Didn't care for the offer?"

"More that he didn't care for mine." At Emery's look, she shrugged. "My mother was sick and I wanted to take care of her and my father. I suggested he come with me."

"And?"

"And..." she shrugged again. "He said no."

A moment passed before Emery said, "I'm sorry."

"I was, too."

And they spoke no more until they arrived at the Skinner house.

***

The Skinners's lake house was a large log cabin at the end of a long drive. The driveway was smooth gravel, the lawns immaculately cut, and the gardens fragrant and well-tended. When Mrs. Skinner, a short, plump woman with stylishly cut gray hair and a motherly face, welcomed them inside, they saw that the rustic exterior was misleading. The Skinners had money and liked all the modern conveniences.

She led them into a spacious and comfortable living room, with large windows overlooking the lake. Outside, sparkling in the late afternoon sun, the water lapped gently around a dock. A small sail boat and a mid-sized motor boat with fishing tackle stowed neatly on it, rocked on either side. Two thin, tan boys in swimming trunks and loose shirts, were jumping off the dock into the water.

"My grandsons," Mrs. Skinner said happily,

when she saw Emery watching them. "They're up from Andover this week for a visit. The youth always give one hope, don't they?"

"Yes, ma'am," Emery said and turned from the window. "I hope we haven't interrupted a family event."

She waved her hand dismissively. "Oh, don't you worry. We have them all week and I'm sure they appreciate the break from being with their old grandparents. Do you have children?"

Mrs. Skinner looked from him to Norah, clearly thinking they were together. Emery waited for Norah to correct her, but all she said was, "No, but I like them."

"Children are wonderful," she said happily. "Just don't wait too long to start, dear. The energy one needs to keep up!" She shook her head and chuckled, oblivious to Norah's blushing discomfort. "Anyway, you arrived at a good time. Otis has just come in. He's changing now, but if you'll wait, he'll be right down to see you. Are you... friends of his?"

It was her first betrayal of any curiosity.

"My father was a patient at his clinic," Norah

said quietly. "I was just wondering if he could help me with some information."

The expression on Mrs. Skinner's face changed from friendly openness to a sympathetic kind of pity. She nodded knowingly.

"Then he'll probably talk to you in the study," she said. "But please, make yourself at home here until he comes down. I was just about to have some lemonade. Would you like some?"

"Please," Emery said.

She bustled out into the kitchen. Judging from the smells and sounds emanating from that direction, she wasn't the one doing the cooking.

Norah nervously paced back and forth. Emery stepped closer and dropped his voice.

"It's going to be all right, Norah," he said. "Whatever it is, we can handle it."

She stopped her nervous movement for a moment, her eyes on his. Then her shoulders slumped.

"You mean, me," she said. "I'll be the one who has to handle it. Alone. Which I will. It's just..."

Mrs. Skinner came in then, bearing a tray of lemonade and four crystal glasses that glinted in the sun pouring through the big windows. She was followed closely by a man just her age, with a gray fringe of hair, kindly eyes, and a welcoming smile. His balding pate was pale, but the face beneath it was red from the sun and contrasted with his sharp blue eyes.

"Hello, hello," he said and offered his hand to shake. "How are you? Emery, right? I'm Doctor Skinner. Margaret tells me that your father was a client of mine."

He had a good firm grip and didn't seem at all surprised or discomforted when Emery redirected him towards Norah.

"My father," she said, also shaking his hand. "It was some time ago."

"I see," he said. "And is your father well?"

When Norah hesitated and looked at Emery, Mrs. Skinner said, "Why don't you show this young couple your office, Otis? It'll be quieter in there and the view is very nice this time of year."

"Of course." Otis gestured. "If you'll come with me, Mrs. Emery?"

Norah didn't look at Emery now.

They followed Doctor Skinner down a short hall into a mid-sized room, lined with half-filled bookshelves and dominated by an enormous oak desk. There was a fire place against one wall, a few chairs, and a large window behind the desk. It allowed for plenty of light and showed almost the exact same view as the living room.

Doctor Skinner shut the door and gestured them towards the two chairs in front of the desk. He settled himself behind it and took a sip of his lemonade. Norah took one of the chairs, but Emery chose to stand behind her. Despite Captain Donovan's insistence on his involvement, this was still essentially a family affair.

"Now then, Mrs. Emery," the doctor began, but Norah cut him off.

"It's Donovan," she said. "Miss Norah Donovan. My father is Captain Harry Donovan, of Portsmouth."

Recognition rippled across the doctor's face and he nodded solemnly.

"Oh, yes," he said softly. "Captain Donovan. I remember him very well. A talkative man. Always told the very best stories. All of my nurses loved him. Yes, I see the resemblance now."

"Thank you."

"I remember your mother, too. A lovely woman. How is she?"

"She passed away a year ago."

His eyes sharpened. "I see." After a moment, he asked, "And how is your father? As I recall, he was released quite some time ago."

Norah glanced up at Emery. She unconsciously twisted the glass in her hands.

"I guess… I guess that's what we wanted to talk to you about, Doctor," she said. "You see… I just learned that he was in your clinic and that information – well, it surprised me."

Doctor Skinner nodded. "Most people are embarrassed to admit that they needed treatment," he said gently. "It's nothing that one needs to be ashamed of. Even the strongest soul needs rest and a retreat from time to time. But an independent man like your father would have had difficulty admitting that he even needed a rest, let alone anything else."

"*Was* there anything else?" she asked. When Doctor Skinner glanced at Emery warningly, she said, "You can speak freely in front of Mr. Emery – he's a family friend and has my father's blessing."

Doctor Skinner hesitated. Then the role of man-at-ease slipped away and he was a confidential, competent doctor. He put his glass on the desk and leaned forward, steepling his hands as he concentrated. Emery got the impression that this was his favorite pose when trying to reassure family members.

"You're aware of the circumstances surrounding your father's admittance into my sanitarium?" he asked.

"I know that it occurred in conjunction with the death of his friend at sea, yes."

"Terrible thing, that accident," Skinner said. "It would have been painful enough even if Jasper Smith hadn't been a close friend."

Norah started in surprise and Emery said, with some suspicion, "You have a good memory, Doctor. Captain Donovan was admitted almost ten years ago."

Skinner looked up at him, his eyes twinkling. "I have an excellent memory, Mr. Emery, but not that good." He looked at Norah. "I saw the article in the paper a week or two ago and your father's name reminded me of the case. I pulled his file in the clinic. In fact..." he reached into the drawer and pulled out a worn file, thick with yellowing papers, "I brought it with me."

"That was...lucky," Norah said. She sounded as suspicious as Emery felt.

The doctor chuckled and dropped the file on the table. "Not really. I thought perhaps the local authorities might be calling on me. They haven't, by the way, and I should tell you that there's little I can tell them, bound by oath as I am. Your father's file is safe with me."

Then why bring it? Emery thought, but what Norah asked was, "You can guess why I'm here then, doctor."

"Of course." He tapped the file and smiled. "You want to know what my diagnosis was."

"Yes."

She sounded stiff, as though preparing herself for the worst. Emery found his hand on her shoulder before he knew what he was doing, but she didn't flinch from his touch. If anything, she relaxed into it.

The doctor looked at her in a fatherly manner, a manner so much a well-practiced act that Emery decided on the spot that, should the diagnosis be the worst, Captain Donovan was never going back into Doctor Skinner's control.

"Miss Donovan," the doctor said. "I can't give you all the details of your father's state of mind at the time of his treatment, but I can tell you this: he was suffering from acute guilt and a nervous collapse. We treated him for both of those things and let him go home in his wife's care."

"So..." Norah sounded cautiously hopeful. "So he wasn't... crazy?"

"I don't like to use such terms, Miss Donovan."

"What term would you prefer?" Emery asked sharply.

The doctor raised an eyebrow at him and Norah's hand gently covered his own.

"Was he delusional, then?" she asked calmly.

Doctor Skinner looked at his file. "It is natural that, when an accident of such devastation occurs, that the mind tries to correct the story to relieve the sufferer of guilt or blame. Mr. Smith was a family man and left small children behind. Your father felt responsible for both his loss and their suffering, but of course, it *was* just an accident. The sea was harsh, the winds were bad, and Mr. Smith was drunk. Captain Donovan was no more responsible than the boat itself."

"But that story…"

The doctor's eyes glittered. "He told you, then?"

She nodded and gained strength. "Yes. About the catch and… the creatures."

"I see. And when did he tell you this?"

"Just the other day."

"After the article was released and after his heart attack?"

"Yes."

"Were you with him when your mother died, Miss Donovan?"

Her grip on Emery's hand tightened. "Yes I was."

"How did your father react?"

"He was heartbroken, of course. Grieving."

"How did that grief express itself?"

"He was quiet and became withdrawn. My mother was ill for a long time, so it was almost a relief when she passed, but still… it hurt him. He – he drank, too, until I convinced him to stop."

"When was that?"

"About three months after her death. He hadn't touched a drop until..." She stopped, as though she'd said too much.

The doctor looked at her sharply.

"When did he start drinking again, Miss Donovan?"

She licked her lips and said, in a soft voice, "About a month ago – when he came back from Portsmouth with the Jensen boat."

"And is that when he first started talking about monsters?"

"Y-yes."

"All right, doctor," Emery said, allowing his annoyance into his tone. "Now that you've given Miss Donovan the third degree, would you mind answering *her* questions?"

"Of course," Doctor Skinner leaned back in his chair, steepling his hands again. "Let me be blunt with the pair of you. You came here today wondering if the stories in the newspapers were true – that your father is suffering from delusions. Isn't that right, Miss Donovan?"

She lifted her chin and said, "Yes."

"Well, the truth of the matter is, I don't know,

Miss Donovan. I can't diagnose a man long distance. But what I can tell you is this: judging from what you've told me and from what my notes were when your father first came to me, there is a chance, a chance mind you, that he is about to suffer a relapse. It's possible that he has been unable to grieve your mother's death and that his unfortunate decision to travel back to the scene of Jasper Smith's accident triggered his old complaint and that, if I'm right, without rest and the right kind of care, his inability to face the tragedies of life may in turn cause a mental collapse. This is, of course," he repeated gently, "all hypothesis. Without an examination, I can make no positive claim."

Norah was trembling under Emery's hand. "Do you think he's... dangerous?" she asked.

Doctor Skinner's gaze was steady. "I couldn't say for sure," he said. "Tell me, what does he think ought to be done about the creatures in the lake, Miss Donovan?"

His expression was almost cruel, with its frigid, unyielding authority.

Norah swallowed hard.

"He hasn't said, Doctor." Her voice was small.

The doctor's eyes glinted. "Well, now," he said softly. "That in itself is interesting. If a man thought he was in true danger, the obvious answer would be to run or face it. But facing it might mean facing the truth about himself. Do you understand me, Miss Donovan?"

Norah nodded, but could say nothing more. Her trembling increased, as did Emery's agitation. He tightened his grip on her shoulder and said, coldly, "I appreciate your openness, doctor. Can I ask a question: has a man called Phillip Cabot called to ask you about Captain Donovan?"

The doctor frowned. "No... Though the name is familiar."

"His father arranged for the captain's original treatment."

"Ah! But the answer is still the same. No one named Cabot has come asking any questions."

"Has the sheriff?" Norah asked. "Sheriff Young?"

"No."

"That's a relief," Norah sighed and lowered her head into her hands.

She looked done in and Emery wished he hadn't

thought to take her along, even if her presence was necessary to get the answers from the doctor.

I could have lied, he thought, and just as he was about to make their excuses to leave, Doctor Skinner spoke up.

Doctor Skinner said, in a tone meant to comfort, "We are very confidential, Miss Donovan, and your parents were quite insistent that only family know of his stay with us. I think your parents, Mr. Cabot, you and your brother are the only ones who know of his treatment. Well, and Mr. Emery now of course..."

Norah's head snapped up and she stared at the doctor in horror. "My brother?"

For once, Doctor Skinner looked unsure.

"Yes," he said, looking from her to Emery and back again. "He called me the other day, asking the same questions. Said his name was Jeremy Donovan, that he was worried about his father, that he was concerned for your welfare, seeing as you were living in the same house. That's why I was so surprised when Margaret told me you were coming. I thought for sure he would tell you himself. Didn't he tell you we talked?"

Norah rose, steady and icily calm.

"I don't see how he could, Doctor Skinner," she said coldly. "He's been dead for twelve years."

She left the room without saying another word.

***

"It *had* to be Philip." Norah's voice was taut and cold with anger. She drummed her long fingers on the door handle as she watched the scenery pass by. "Who else could it have been?"

"One of his city friends maybe." Emery kept his voice as level as her's.

She gave him a sidelong look. "Do you *really* think that?"

He shook his head. "No."

"Neither do I." She looked out the window again. "How could he *do* this to Father?"

Emery didn't answer and she said nothing more. He drove steadily, keeping one eye on the road and the other on her, noticing the silent way she brushed the tears away. She hadn't said a word to the Skinners when they left, leaving Emery to thank the doctor and refuse Mrs. Skinner's invitation to stay for dinner. Doctor Skinner's oily confidence had been shaken when he realized that he'd been fooled by "Jeremy Donovan". He'd seemed as relieved to see them go as they'd been to get on the road.

Norah's voice was cold when she said: "When I see Philip Cabot, I'll kill him."

14

Norah did not have long to wait to see Philip again. When they pulled into the driveway, Philip's shiny car was sitting there, quiet and cold. It was dusk and moths and bats were just starting to come out of their hiding places to test the new night air. The house was mostly dark, with the only light pouring from the kitchen and dining room area.

Fido raced out to meet them, barking in a warning manner, but he needn't have bothered. Norah had already slammed her door with unnecessary force and was storming into the house, her face black with fury.

Emery was only a half-step behind, but that was enough for Norah to beat him to the back porch. She was standing in the doorway, hands on her hips. A half-drunk Philip Cabot grinned up at her from his deck chair, his hands wrapped around a glass with only a drop of alcohol left in it. Fido nervously paced around her, looking from Philip, to Philip's two city friends and back again.

"Norah, darling!" Philip was saying, as Emery appeared in the doorway. "Where *have* you two been keeping yourselves?"

Philip, the city men, and Captain Donovan were sitting around the porch table. Despite it's being so warm that Philip was down to his shirt-sleeves, the city men kept their jackets on and closed in front. Donovan was still in his hunting clothes. His glass was nearly full and his flushed face and the lethargic manner in which he slumped spoke of his inebriation. The two city men had drinks, but they were too professional to be drunk. Even Philip was only acting. His eyes, even in the dying light, were too sharp for a wasted man.

The city men noticed Emery first and adjusted their positions accordingly, accidentally giving Emery a fleeting glimpse of a leather shoulder holster. Their movement drew Philip's attention and he said loudly, "Chief! Won't you join us for a drink?"

Donovan stirred then and looked at Emery, blinking.

"Philip Cabot!" Norah exclaimed. "What do you think you are doing?"

Philip looked at her, all innocence.

"Having a drink with a few of my friends," he said sweetly.

"Having a *drink*?!"

"It isn't illegal any more. Why don't you join us? And the chief is welcome, too, of course."

She took a step closer and glared down at him. "You *know* my father has only just recently been released from the hospital. Drinking is the *worst* thing for him."

Again, he blinked back up at her, all innocence.

"He didn't object when we offered him a glass, did he boys?"

The two city men shook their heads, looking amused. Norah looked ready to fly off the handle then, something that would be unwise in front of the city men. So Emery stepped in and put his hand on her shoulder, effectively stopping her tirade before it started.

"Why don't we get your father inside and get some coffee into him, Norah? It's getting late."

She hesitated, then nodded. Giving Philip one last, withering look, she turned to her father. Donovan hadn't done anything to acknowledge their arrival. He sat motionless, staring at his shoes in drunken contemplation and only stirred when Norah took his arm. He was too heavy for her to lift herself, so Emery turned back to Philip.

"Help her," he said.

Philip might have objected, but Emery's look and tone, honed like a fine-edged sword after years of commanding crewmen, brooked no refusal. He put down his glass and shoved himself out of the chair. He took Donovan's arm with a merry, "Come along, old man. Time to get you some coffee!"

Emery stood aside to allow the three of them through the porch door. Fido followed them to the doorway, then stopped and looked up at Emery, his tail wagging. Emery grinned at him, then turned to the city men. They hadn't moved since Emery's arrival and were regarding him now, one with cool discernment, the other with amusement.

"Gentlemen," Emery said. "I don't wish to be rude, but Captain Donovan has had enough excitement tonight. I trust you understand."

The words were polite and the tone was unmistakable. One of the city men, the passenger he'd seen earlier, raised an eyebrow.

"Only been here a day and already you run a tight ship, sailor," he observed.

Emery leaned against the door, running his hat through his hands, regarding them with the same cool interest. Although he almost was sure he wouldn't need it, he wished he was wearing his pistol, too.

"Who told you I was only here a day?" he asked, with mild interest.

The other man shrugged.

"Something the old man said. He said you were here working for him. He didn't say in what capacity. Made me and Alph curious. What work would there be up here for a man of your skills?"

"Funny," Emery said quietly. "But I was just thinking the same about you two."

The smile broadened. "Oh, we're just here for the sights."

"Are you? Well, I've heard Holloway is nice this time of year. So is Laconia."

The smile tightened. After a beat, the city man raised his glass to Emery. "I think we've worn out our welcome, Alph."

"Yeah," said Alph. He didn't look as affable now.

The city man drained his glass and then deliberately placed his cup on the table. As one, he and Alph stood, adjusting their jackets, looking at Emery as though from a great height, even though they were the same size. "It's been a pleasure, Chief," the city man said. "Maybe we'll run into you in town."

"Maybe," Emery said.

The city man nodded. "Tell Phil we'll be in touch."

"I'll do that."

They nodded. Emery didn't move from the doorway, so after a momentary pause, the city man smiled knowingly. He and Alph walked down from the porch and around the house.

As Emery watched them go, Norah appeared in the doorway. She was about to speak, but he shook his head. He slipped past her into the house and looked out the kitchen window. Alph was leaning into Emery's car, checking the sunscreens and the glove compartment while the other stood by Philip's car, lighting up. When Alph came up empty handed, the cigarette smoking mobster shrugged and they climbed into their car and drove off.

"Who *are* they?"

Norah's voice came from right by Emery's elbow. He shook his head and allowed the curtain to fall back into place.

"I don't know," he said. "But they're dangerous."

"How dangerous?"

"I don't know." He stepped away, rubbing his face. "How's your father?"

"I think he's okay. He really shouldn't be drinking like this. His heart is..."

"I know," Emery said.

They heard a step and turned to see Philip stagger into the room, one hand in his pocket, and the other wrapped around the nearly empty bottle of bourbon.

"You really know how to ruin a party, Norah, darling," he started.

Norah's temper snapped. She stormed over to him and, eyes flashing, slapped his face.

The sound echoed throughout the kitchen and, judging from way Philip's head whipped about, it was a good, hefty blow.

"Philip Cabot!" she hissed. "You *really* are a dirty, rotten snake in the grass!"

"Why, Norah!" He sounded astonished. He rubbed his cheek in shock. "What has gotten into you?"

"You – you - !"

She lifted her hand again. Philip jumped back nimbly and put the table between them. Norah darted after him, but Philip was too quick and in a moment, his back was to Emery, the table once again between him and his cousin.

"Chief!" he said. "Aren't you going to do something?"

"I think the lady has a grievance," Emery said laconically.

"I ought to call the police on you, Philip Cabot," Norah hissed. She was furiously angry, her rage bubbling out of her, but still she kept her voice lowered out of concern for her father. "I ought to sue you for invasion of privacy and emotional damage!"

"Norah, darling..."

"Don't you *darling* me, you snake in the grass!"

She lunged, he dodged, and then there they were, facing each other on opposite sides of the table again.

"Chief, I beg you!" Philip cried out.

This time, Emery stepped forward, folding his arms.

"I think you'd better come clean, Cabot," he said softly. "She knows too much now."

"Too much about what?" Philip whined.

Norah snapped, "About Doctor Skinner, you bald-faced liar!"

And just like that, all posturing left Philip's frame. For a split second, he stared at her in open-faced surprise, without any subterfuge and it was clear to everyone in the room, that the idea that she might discover his duplicity before his plan had worked out had never once crossed his mind.

But it was over in a moment. The steel trap shut

again and he was all motion and oily protestations of innocence. "Norah, Norah, how you misunderstand me!"

"Misunderstand!" she shrieked in a whisper. "Somehow you found out about my father's visit to Doctor Skinner's rest home and then you *pretend* to be *my dead brother* to get information out of him, private information. Personal information, information even I didn't know."

"It was for his own good…"

"Don't, Philip!" She threw up her hands then. "Just don't! I can't take one more lie."

"It was! Darling, I saw the state your father was in and I knew how painful it was for you. So I called Doctor Skinner to see if I could learn anything that might be helpful. Why bother you, when you were already overwhelmed by these distressing circumstances?"

"And did you?" Emery asked. When Philip looked at him, he finished, "Find anything helpful?"

Philip deliberately hesitated. "Not… exactly."

"You mean," Norah leaned in, her expression sharp. "That you didn't find anything to help *you.*

Nothing you could take to the sheriff to ensure that my father goes to the asylum for insanity! You want this house and the only way you can drive my father out of it is to declare him insane!"

Now Philip drew himself up in well-defined outrage. "That is an outrageous suggestion!" he sputtered. "I'm insulted. I'm offended. That you would think that I, your cousin, your childhood companion, would stoop so low as to try to…"

"How much to do you owe Alph and his friend?" Emery cut in.

Philip stopped mid-sentence and blinked. Then he raised his chin and took a step towards Emery, outrage and indignation fairly flowing out of every pore. He was, Emery admitted to himself ruefully, a very good actor. If, indeed, he was acting. But even as the doubt crossed his mind, a flicker of an expression ran across Philip's soft features and Emery knew that his instincts were dead on. The man was lying.

"That," Philip said levelly, "is a private affair."

Emery held his gaze. "So is her father's medical condition."

The other man grinned. "The sheriff may argue with you there."

"Get out," Norah hissed from across the table. Both men turned to look at her. She was pale and shaking, holding on to the table with a white-knuckled grip. When she spoke, it was through teeth gritted so tight, it was amazing that any sound could emit at all. "Get out of my house, Philip, before I throw you out."

Philip looked at her, then at Emery, and his eyes narrowed as he turned back to his cousin.

"Your house?" he asked mildly.

Norah started as if to tear across the table, but he took a half step back and raised one warning finger. "I'll go, I'll go. I have an appointment in town at eleven o'clock anyway."

"Get *out*!" she cried low as though in pain.

Philip looked to Emery. "I don't suppose I could borrow your car?" he asked. At Emery's side-long look, he sighed. "I'll take a bike then."

"You can *walk*," Norah snapped. "I'll send your things to the hotel later."

For a moment, Emery thought that Philip was going to protest again. His shoulders went back, his head came up, and he stepped towards her as though to reassert his ownership. But he *didn't* actually own the house. No one really did. That was the crux of the whole thing and everyone in that room knew it. So with a sigh, Philip took his hat from the peg in the wall and dropped it on his head.

"I'll go to the Blue House to sleep this off," he said, archly, as though he were the wounded party. "When you've calmed down, Norah, we'll have a good long talk."

"Get. Out."

Suddenly, from overhead, there came a heavy thud and a moaning cry of pain, followed by Fido's warning bark. Norah's head snapped to attention, and then she fled up the stairs, calling, "Father!"

Philip took a half step after her, but Emery stopped him by placing a hand on his shoulder.

"I think that's your cue to exit, brother," he said.

The smaller man turned to give Emery a searching look. Overheard, they heard Norah's soothing murmurs, followed by another protesting groan from the captain.

"I don't know what your game here is, Captain,"

Philip said. "But you should probably know – Norah has nothing. She'll have even less when the captain passes away or..." and his grin sharpened, "moves on. You're wasting your time. Not to mention, interfering in what is *purely* a family matter. Those who step in the middle of a battle tend to get caught in the crossfire. Do the right thing. Stay out of this."

Emery just managed to keep his fists at his side.

"Cabot," he said. "The door is that way."

Philip's grin didn't even slip a notch. He threw his hands up as if in surrender, then moved towards the door. "Just don't say I didn't warn you, Captain."

He didn't leave a moment too soon. Emery stood in the middle of the dining room, willing his temper back into control. Then he moved to check the window. Philip was disappearing around the bend in the road. Only then did Emery go upstairs to help Norah put her drunken father back into his bed.

***

Captain Donovan was in a querulous mood and Norah was remote with anger. She looked after her father with the tenderness of a mother looking after a recalcitrant child. Emery left her to it and went back downstairs with Fido. He made sandwiches for both him and Norah, fed the dog, and then went outside on the porch to sit in the gathering gloom and think. Fido joined him after a bit and they were still sitting there when Norah came out sometime later. She was carrying Philip's suitcase.

"I'm throwing him out," she said. "I'll not tolerate someone like that under my roof while my father is in such a state."

"All right," Emery replied. "Do you want me to bring that to the hotel?"

She looked relieved. "Would you?"

"Better than him coming here."

"Much. I hate to ask, but I don't want to leave Father alone right now. The Blue House is right in town."

Emery rose from his chair and took the bag. "I'll do it. I want to talk to him anyway."

"Charles..." She stopped him with a touch on

the arm. "You... don't need to talk to him. It's a family matter and I..."

He covered her hand with his own and squeezed it.

"I'll just bring him his bag," he said.

She smiled and he left her, feeling only slightly guilty that he'd lied to her about his true intentions.

"I'll go, Norah, I'll go. I have an appointment in town anyway tonight."

Philip had an appointment in town that night and Emery had a pretty good idea who it was with.

The Blue House was an over-grown salt shaker on the edge of the lake with a wide drive and a well-lit sign that proclaimed "Vacancy". A succession of small blue cottages trailed along the left of the house. The neatly tended front lawn and the tidy garden that graced the right side of the house contrasted sharply with the buildings' need for a fresh coat of paint. The front office only furthered the impression: it was neat as a pin and clean, but several years past a need for an update.

When Emery rang the desk bell, a stout woman, neatly but simply dressed, stepped out of a side room. A swirl of scent – pot roast and coffee – came with her.

"Need a room?" she asked. She had a square

face and pallid blue eyes, but her strong arms spoke of hard work and determination.

Emery placed the suitcase on the desk. "I'm looking for Philip Cabot," he said. "I was told he might be here."

Her eyes narrowed. "Who's asking?"

"Norah Donovan." When she blinked in recognition, he explained, "I'm Emery. Miss Donovan asked me to deliver Cabot's suitcase to him."

Her suspicion cleared a little. "So they've been fighting? That explains it. He came in here an hour ago, dusty and just coming off a hangover. Wouldn't explain to me, just went off with Harry."

"Harry?"

"My husband. They went to school together." She reached for the handle. "I'll take this."

He put his hand on the suitcase. "I don't mind delivering it," he said easily.

Another look of suspicion.

"I don't give out guest information," she said. "Especially to people I don't know. You can leave this with me and tell Norah I took care of it."

"I have a message for Philip. Is he here?"

"You can write it down and I'll give it to him."

"Is he here?"

"He's not. Write it down." She slid a pad of paper and a pencil across the counter.

Emery cocked his head at her. "Are you always so cautious about your guests' privacy?"

She leveled a look at him. "Certain guests, yes. I don't want trouble on my property. Philip Cabot doesn't always bring out the best in people."

Emery had to laugh at that. "So I noticed." He slid the suitcase towards her. She took it and gave him a second look.

"Norah really sent you?"

"As God is my witness."

She hesitated, then said, "Look, I don't want trouble."

"So you've said. I'm not looking for trouble. I just want some answers." After a moment, he said, "I guess I can wait in my car until Philip returns..."

That resolved her unspoken dilemma.

"You might try the pub on Elm Street," she said. "They didn't say where they were going, but Philip usually ends up there."

"For the atmosphere?"

She raised an eyebrow. "For the cards."

He nodded and smiled at her. "Thank you, ma'am."

"Tell Harry Irene said to come home."

"I will."

He left the motel, leaving Irene alone in a tidy, lonely office.

***

The pub on Elm Street was conveniently called The Pub on Elm Street and it was only one street over from the diner where Emery first stopped in town. Though it was only about nine o'clock, the street was quiet and dark and the Pub was one of only a few places open. Emery parked the car two streets away and walked back to the entrance. Then, adjusting his hat so that it covered his face a little more, he went inside.

The interior was restfully dark, with a once-posh, now well-worn red carpet and furniture made of dark wood. There were two layers of tables scattered around the room and an enormous bar lined one of the walls. It was crowded, with a mix of better-dressed out-of-towners, desperately looking for alcoholic relief from the peaceful boredom of a lake town, and the locals, whose rougher dress and careless carriage spoke of other problems. A small band played in one corner and three couples were slowly moving across the floor, two in time with the beat, the third so drunk they'd nearly forgotten why they were there. The room was loud with talk and laughter and no one particularly noticed Emery.

He stood in the darkness of the doorway, scanning the room, but neither Philip Cabot nor the two city boys were in attendance. He checked his watch again. It was 9:15 and Emery wondered if Philip was telling the truth about his appointment. If not, Emery was wasting his time. But there was no point in worrying about that. He had nothing better to do, other than sitting at Donovan's lake house, seething.

He was about to leave when a shriek of laughter coming from somewhere up above him caught his attention. There was a staircase on his right, shrouded in shadows and now Emery realized that music and laughter was also drifting in from above.

He remembered what Irene said about the card games and took the steps two at a time.

The stairway terminated in a doorway, where a large, laconic man in a rumpled suit sat at a tiny table with a half-drunken beer. He stood the minute Emery appeared.

"What do you want?" he asked.

Behind him, the sounds of laughter and gambling were clear. Emery pulled out his wallet.

"Thought I might join in on the fun," he said.

The doorman hesitated, then shook his head.

"I don't know you," he said. "And this," he jerked his head towards the door, "is a private party."

He shifted in his stance and flexed his big hands. It was clear that he was itching to be a gangster like in the movies.

Emery shrugged and peeled off a ten. "Where can one get an invite?"

The doorman just looked at him.

"Private party," he repeated. "And I don't know you, sir."

Emery might have pushed the matter harder, had he not heard the ringing sound of Philip's mocking laughter echoing throughout the room. It was so loud that even the doorman started and looked to the door as though expecting someone or something to burst through it.

"That!" Philip cried out, "is how you keep a poker face, doll!"

A peel of womanly laughter joined his. The doorman shook his head and turned back to find Emery pulling another ten out of his wallet.

"Look, mister," he said in warning, but Emery shook his head and pressed the two bills into the doorman's hand.

"Philip Cabot," he said.

The doorman's eyes narrowed. "Who?"

"You know who. Who is he with?"

The doorman's hands tightened around the bills, but Emery held on to them.

"He came alone," the doorman finally admitted. "He always comes alone."

"There are two strangers in town..."

"More than two, mister."

"Two strangers," Emery said, slowly, firmly. "City men, New York probably. Expensive suits, carrying guns. They were driving Cabot's car to-day. You know who I mean?"

"I saw them. What's this about?"

"Never mind. Are they also at the party?"

"Look, I don't want any trouble."

"I'm not offering any. Are they inside?"

The doorman shook his head. "No. The boss didn't like the look of them, so they never got an invitation."

Emery grinned. "Your boss is particular."

"She's careful," he clarified. "And she doesn't like it when her staff talks to strangers, so why don't you beat it, mister?"

Emery pulled another bill out. "Any chance you could let me know when Cabot leaves?"

"There's only one door here."

"I believe that, like I believe what's going on behind there is a revival meeting."

The doorman grinned briefly, then snatched the bills from Emery's hand. He thrust them into his pocket as Emery watched, then gestured with his chin towards the stairs.

"My boss doesn't like people loitering," he said.

Emery grinned. He felt the man's stare all the way back down the stairs.

16

Emery bought himself a drink and nursed it at the bar for the next hour or so. The music was loud and clamorously bad and the thick air of cigarette smoke made his throat itch. But all things considered, it was a low-key, relaxed crowd, unlike what one would find in the places Emery normally went for late night drinks.

Around ten o'clock, a group of younger people came in, well-dressed and throwing money around like it was going out of style. They were nearly all drunk already. They danced and laughed, drank and smoked. Once, Emery heard them talking about the monster of Deep Water Lake.

"Lord, I wish there *was* a monster!" one of the women complained. "A least *that* would be interesting!"

Time passed by with agonizing slowness. Emery finished one beer and, to keep the bartender from getting too suspicious, ordered another. He kept a half eye on the stairs, and wondered what kind of a fool he was. Surely there was another way upstairs. Perhaps the man – or woman – Cabot was meeting was already in the room. Perhaps the meeting had nothing to do with pressuring Donovan to surrender the lake house. Just how much financial trouble was Philip Cabot in to make the lake house such a priority?

A shriek from one of the young women sliced through Emery's increasingly morbid thoughts and jogged his memory. He recognized her voice as one of the boaters who'd shouted at Donovan. Now when he glanced at the party, he recognized one of the young men, too.

Some pretty sorry lives, he thought sourly. *Getting their kicks tormenting crazy old men.*

The woman was seriously drunk now. She playfully fought her way off of a young man's lap, her happy, flirty tones belying her struggle. Finally free, she staggered over to the bar, still laughing, and her unfocused gaze lit upon Emery.

"Well!" she said, delighted, her tone slurred with drink. "All alone, honey? Buy Mama a drink and I'll keep you company."

Emery shrugged. "Sorry, Mama," he said. "I'm fresh out of cash."

"A charity case, huh?" Giggling, she threw a bill at the bartender and fell into one of the stools. "That's alright, Sugar. I've got enough for two, maybe three."

She leaned in on Emery, giving him a whiff of fading perfume and stale alcohol. Her eyes, he noted, were large and luminous. She was a young woman, made old and tired by the situation. Her makeup was thick and starting to run in the heat. Her platinum blonde hair and fashionably slinky outfit were designed to entice and allure, but when Emery looked at her, all he could see was her youth and her boredom. He felt old and exhausted suddenly and that irritated him.

He glanced at his watch and saw that the time was ten to eleven. He got up off of the stool and was reaching for his wallet when she stopped him, grabbing his arm.

"Come on, stranger," she slurred. "Take a risk."

The hand was small, the arm wasted from ill-use and possibly substance abuse. But her nails were impeccable.

Emery shrugged her off and growled: "Why don't you go home, kid? Life's too short to waste."

Her wide eyes narrowed. "Pig!" she snarled.

Her hand flashed, but she was drunk and the slap had little power. One of the girls in her set began to laugh hysterically. Emery stepped back as the bartender inserted himself into the situation.

"Come on, Diana," he said. "Let's not have any trouble tonight, all right?"

He turned her and pushed her back towards her group of friends, who immediately began to argue with him. Emery grabbed his hat and was turning to leave when suddenly, Philip appeared in the gloom of the stairs.

Emery immediately turned back to the bar. Through the barroom mirror, he saw Philip pause at the bottom of the stairs to light a cigarette. The commotion from the rich kids, now trying to convince the bartender that if he wouldn't throw Emery out, he ought to at least buy the next round, drew his attention only for a moment. Philip eyed the girls, drew in a cloud of smoke, then tossed the match and turned towards the door. From the way he adjusted his jacket and the lackluster tilt of his hat, Philip Cabot hadn't won tonight either.

He went out the back way and then the doorman appeared in the stairway. He nodded to Emery, who lifted a hand in thanks. He waited a few moments before following Philip outside.

The air outside was dark and sultry. Emery immediately stepped out of the light of the open door into the shadows. It took a moment for his eyes to adjust to the darkness. When they did, he saw Philip, now on the other side of Elm, walking down the alleyway, kicking at some garbage. He was heading towards the lake.

Emery followed, keeping close to the shadows. Philip reached Main Street, and paused, looking longingly up the street at something. Then, with a sigh, he crossed Main, turned south, and began to walk in the general direction of the diner. Emery stayed on the opposite side, hidden in the shadows. When he glanced north, he saw what Philip was sighing after: his car sat quiet and sleek, glinting in the semi-circle of light cast by the hotel windows.

It was, Emery had to admit, a fine looking vehicle, even in repose.

Philip had nearly reached the empty diner now, but instead of crossing in front of it, he turned and disappeared down the narrow alley alongside of it. Emery crossed the road and stuck to the shadows, running lightly until he reached the alley way. He paused before peering into the alley. Philip was already several yards away, difficult to see in the shadows. Emery slipped into the alley, staying close to the wall of the diner where the shadows were thickest. Philip paused. Emery slipped into a recessed doorway in the wall and watched.

Quiet washed over him. Now Emery could hear the sound of the lake water, lapping up against the docks just a few hundred yards away and the boats bumping up against their moorings. The scent of lake water mingled with that of the rubbish that moldered in tin cans very near where the two men stood and waited.

For Philip was obviously waiting for someone. He turned and leaned against the opposite wall, almost disappearing into the shadows. The sharp sound of a striking match and the quick flash of flame told Emery that he was prepared to wait a little time. But why here, in the dark? Why not in the hotel, where the two city men were already comfortably ensconced? Or in the Pub, where no one but the jealous doorman and his prickly boss would particularly care?

It was then that Emery first heard a small, scratching noise, like someone missing a lock with their key and hitting wood instead. It sounded hollow, like an echo, and distant, perhaps from somewhere around the corner and out of sight. He craned to look, but the sound ceased.

Philip hadn't appeared to notice. He smoked his cigarette in peaceable silence and glanced at his watch. From overhead, someone in one of the top floor rooms of the building opposite began to play jazz softly and down the street, a woman's tinkling, drunken laughter echoed down the street. Deep Water was quiet compared to New York City or Boston, but it still had a form of night life.

Emery heard footsteps and the mutter of voices on Main Street and instantly pressed himself tighter into the darkness of the doorway. He wasn't a moment too soon, too, for almost as soon as he did, two men appeared at the end of the alleyway. It was then that Emery heard the second sound. This one was light, like glass breaking and it came from inside the diner behind him. But he was fairly trapped – if he moved, he'd give himself away.

The two men heard it, too. Their heads swiveled and their hands went inside their coats. A familiar voice said, "Hey! It's Phil."

Another said, "Well, speak of the devil himself."

At the other end of the alley, Philip's shoulders slumped. The two city men stepped into the shadows. Emery caught the scent of expensive cologne as they brushed past him. Inside the diner, against his ear on the wall, he heard the faint sounds of footsteps across the cheap flooring.

In the alley, the two gangsters drew up on Philip, spreading slightly, pinning him in place against the wall.

"What gives, Cabot?" The gangster's silky voice floated quietly above the distance jazz.

Philip didn't exactly sound pleased. "What are you two doing here?"

"We saw you as we were passing by, thought

we'd say hi," was the drawling reply. "When do we get the rest of our money, Phil?"

"I told you, I'll have it all as soon as I get the old man off of my property. You've got to give me a little more time."

"Easy, Phil, easy. We're just protecting our investment. Wanted to make sure you weren't racking up other debts, if you know what I mean."

"I'm not."

"Someone told Alph you were at the Pub. I hope you weren't gambling again, Phil."

Annoyed, Philip flicked away his cigarette. "I got a drink. Anyway, I'm not there now. I'm meeting someone."

"Oh, really?" There was a leer in the gangster's tone.

Philip said quickly, "It's not a woman." When Alph laughed, he snapped: "It's my contact. He was supposed to get the old man out, only..."

"Only he didn't deliver." The gangster sounded thoughtful. "Maybe I should have a talk with this guy."

Philip's voice lost its strength. "I can handle it, Vinny."

"Can you, though? I wonder. I think Alph and I'll wait."

Just then, the third sound came, only this time it was louder. Someone had knocked over something in the diner.

All three men turned and Alph swore.

"What was that?" Vinny asked.

Another sound came from the alley behind them. Alph shouted in triumph and dove. Philip squawked. When Alph returned, he was holding up an emaciated figure in a navy and yellow sweater.

"This who we're waiting for?" Alph asked. The man in his grasp cringed and shrunk away.

"Yes," Philip said, sounding unsure. "Look, fellows, I…"

There was another thud from inside the restaurant, only this time, it was immediately followed by the ringing sound of Sheriff Young's voice: "Who's in there? Come on out!"

"Shoot," said Alph.

"Phil!" said Vinny.

"I didn't!" protested Philip.

The noise of panicked chaos came from inside.

Someone gave up on hiding and was ransacking his way out of the place. Young swore, Boone shouted, "Give it up!" and there was banging sound of a door giving away. Emery became aware that the noise was rapidly approaching the door he leaned on.

The shrunken man in Alph's grasp sudden came to life.

"Help! Murder! Police!!" he cried, writhing in drunken panic.

Vinny responded by pulling his gun and bringing it down on the unfortunate's head. The bum collapsed without a squawk.

"Come on!" he barked. "We ain't getting caught here."

Alph grabbed Philip's shoulder and shoved him into the darkness of the alley away from the restaurant. The sound of Deputy Boone's: "Freeze or I'll shoot!" caused the three men to run and disappear into the darkness, leaving the body of the bum behind them.

Emery pushed himself off of the door and was about to follow when the door flew open behind him. For one brief second, he found himself staring in the wide-eyed, panicked face of Tom Murphy.

"Murphy!" he gasped.

Murphy swung and the lockbox he was carrying connected with Emery's head. The world rocked and stars exploded. The ground rushed up to meet him and somewhere, in the distance, he heard the pounding of Tom Murphy's feet as he raced down the pavement with his stolen goods.

The world steadied and when Emery shook his head, he found himself laying half on the ground, half propped up against the brick wall of the building behind him. A bright light was blinding him, making the searing pain in his head even worse. Emery threw up a hand to block the light.

"Hey!"

Boone's booming voice was threatening. Emery could just make out the wavering outline of the scrawny deputy, holding both the flashlight and a police regulation pistol.

A cacophony of tinny clattering came from down the alley, by the street, where Murphy was desperately hightailing.

Behind Boone, Young's shape loomed.

"Go after him, Boone!" Young scolded.

Boone hesitated, then ran. The light left Emery's eyes, leaving him even more blinded. Boone clattered off down the alley, shouting, and Young bent to look at Emery.

"Hello, Chief," he said. "Now what are you doing here?"

But he was cut off by the ricocheting shot from down the street. Young swore and then he was gone too.

The world rocked, but the pain receded from overwhelming to being merely what had to be the second worst headache of Emery's life. He forced himself upright and felt in his jacket to be sure the pistol was still in its holster. Once reassured, he pushed until he was up on his feet again. The world swam, but he held himself upright and leaned on the brick wall until it steadied again. Then he began to make his way up the alley, towards the bum.

The hobo was lying on his side where the gangsters had left him. Blood stained Captain Donovan's shirt and spattered the gravel around him. He was so still that for a moment, Emery thought the man was dead. But as he stood there, willing the world to still and the ache to fade, he saw the slightest movement of the man's chest. He was not dead. Not yet, anyway.

Philip Cabot, what have you gotten yourself in to?

He carefully lowered himself to his knees beside the prone man, mentally cursing Tom Murphy and his accursed lockbox.

Up close, Emery could now see that the drifter was younger than he'd first supposed. Long exposure to the outdoors, lack of proper food and drink, exhaustion and despair had worn his skin and eaten away at his frame. He was no older than Emery himself, probably younger, and Emery felt, again, the shock of realization. His years at sea and his devotion to the Navy had shielded him from this man's fate.

The drunk moaned again, bring Emery back to his original mission. Dizziness from his head trauma made his vision swim, but he shook off the wave, then gently shook the man. The drunk revived, but his eyes remained closed.

"So thirsty," he muttered, one hand weakly

clutching at Emery's shirt. "Give me something, man…"

"Do you work for Philip Cabot?" Emery asked, low and firm. "Do you?"

"… so thirsty… my head…"

"Philip Cabot! Did he send you to shake up Captain Donovan?"

The drunk's eyes fluttered open.

"The captain," he muttered, then with panic: "The captain!"

His grip on Emery's shirt tightened and twisted and his blue eyes, enormous in his hollowed-out face, were glassy with terror.

"Save him, save him!" he cried.

"Yes." Emery adjusted his grip on the man's shoulders. "You saved him. Did you attack him too?"

"Look out!" the man cried. He was writhing in terror now, looking at something over Emery's shoulder. Emery twisted to look, moving so fast that his head swam again. When his vision cleared, he saw there was nothing but alley behind him and the empty, poorly lit street beyond.

The drunk gasped and collapsed in Emery's

grip. Emery turned back and saw that he had sunken back into a stupor. Annoyed with himself, he shook the man again. "What happened that night?" he asked and shook him again. "Wake up, man, what happened?"

"Emery?"

Sheriff Young's voice echoed in the quiet streets, but Emery was too intent on his prey to answer.

"Answer me!" Emery said. "What did you do to Captain Donovan?"

The man's eyes fluttered and he said weakly, "I tried... I *tried* to save him."

"Did you attack him?"

"I screamed," the man said and closed his eyes again at the memory. "I screamed and... he turned. I threw it at him... I threw the pick but I missed!" His whole body tightened in agony. "I missed! He turned on me – I could see his face... He...! Oh God! Oh God, oh God!"

"Emery!" Young was at the end of the alley now.

The drunk was crying silently, thin shoulders shaking. Emery, disgusted, called out, "I'm here, Sheriff!"

As the sheriff's heavy footsteps echoed towards

them, Emery tried one last time. He shook the man and asked, clearly and slowly: "Did Philip Cabot hire you to attack Captain Donovan?"

But the man only cried out once more, "I tried to save him - but…"

He passed out just as Sheriff Young, perspiring freely and breathless, came up behind Emery to arrest them both.

17

The next few hours were painful chaos. After a short foot chase, the exhausted Murphy surrendered himself and the lock box to Boone and everyone ended up back at the station. Murphy, slumping in defeat and handcuffs in the sheriff office's uncomfortable wooden chairs, admitted readily to the crime.

"I needed the money," he said, looking at his calloused hands, chained together in front of him. "I just needed it, that's all."

He was so sullen that Emery was about to dismiss him as just another violent offender when Young, with uncharacteristic kindness said, "Emily's worse, isn't she, Tom?"

Tom's eyes filled and his mouth pressed tight

against unwarranted emotion. His nod was statement enough.

Young nodded. When Boone hung up from calling one of the town's two doctors, he had the deputy bring Murphy back into the cell while he phoned the owner of the diner. Emery sat in the corner, holding a chunk of ice wrapped in a rag to his head, near where they'd laid the prone drifter. He kept a half an eye on the drifter as he watched as Young gently asked the diner owner to come in.

"There was an incident," he said. "I need you to come in to help me decide what to do about it."

When he hung up, Emery asked, "Isn't breaking and entering a federal offense, Sheriff?"

Sheriff Young gave him an arch look. "So you're a lawyer now, aren't you, Chief?"

"Just a curious citizen."

The sheriff got up and went over to the coffee pot in the corner. "You've been at sea too long, sailor. You haven't been witness to the way things are around here, lately."

"I've seen enough tonight to last me a while, thank you," Emery said.

"I think you haven't," the sheriff said, in his

friendly tone. He poured two cups of coffee and offered one to Emery. "You were probably at sea in '29, right?"

Emery nodded and accepted a cup.

"Right," Young said, "I'll bet you you've seen the papers. But reading about an incident is one thing. Living it's another." He settled back into his desk chair, took a sip of the black, cold brew and went on, conversationally, "Watching a nation deconstruct isn't fun, Chief. Neither is watching men you've known and respected lose everything they'd ever owned or were as men. Not all at once, mind, but slowly. Piece by piece. Slice by slice. Until they were no better off than their parents were, stepping off that boat in rags twenty, thirty years ago. You haven't had to live with the loss of self-respect, the loss of identity. Men like Murphy, they may seem like desperate lowlifes to you. But I remember when he was doing well, went to church, had a wife and family, a pillar in this community. You've only seen what he's become since his job dried up, his wife took the kids to her parents, and his house is about to be lost to the bank. And he's only one man in this one town."

He took another sip and looked at the ceiling. "You haven't had to watch once proud men and women, who'd held their own in self-respect and self-sufficiency, become beggars and worse." He closed his eyes. "I have, Chief. So I can afford to be sympathetic."

There was a moment of silence. Emery, sitting at the edge of the room next to the drifter, felt as foolish and out of touch as he'd ever had.

After enough time had passed for Emery to find himself wishing that Murphy had gotten away with the lock box, Sheriff Young opened his eyes, swung his feet from the desk and leaned forward, ready to work.

"Now, Chief," he said, in a low voice. "Mind telling me what you and your friend were doing out so late in one of our pretty little alley ways?"

***

The sheriff seemed neither surprised nor shocked to learn that Philip Cabot was among the violent offenders. The owner of the diner arrived, looking half-wake and alarmed and was taken into the back with the sheriff to discuss matters. The doctor arrived soon after to look at Emery's head and the drifter. While Emery was deemed well enough – "You've got a hard head, Chief!" - the hobo was in such a state of shock and exhaustion that the doctor insisted he be brought to the hospital.

"He needs food and a long rest," the doctor said. When Young emerged from the back to protest that this man was a key witness in an ongoing investigation, the doctor pushed even harder. "Then you and I both have solid reasons for keeping him alive, don't we, Sheriff?"

It took a long while for the ambulance to arrive from Concord. Though the drifter tossed and muttered in restlessness, he never actually regained consciousness and nothing he said was audible enough to make out. Nothing, that is, until he was actually being loaded into the ambulance and a jolt startled him into shouting: "Stop, oh, stop him stop him stop him!"

The scream was one of pure, unadulterated terror, enough to make Emery's blood run cold.

The doctor, however was sanguine about it.

"There's usually a reason why these drifters hit the bottle," he said. "Like as not, he'll end up in the New Hampshire Hospital or Witcher's before too long."

His cold cynicism was horrifying – and oddly reassuring. It was far too easy, in a remote place like Deep Water where the cold dampness of to-morrow's bad weather was already creeping in over the town, to believe in nightmares.

The ambulance drove off, leaving Emery alone in the darkness of the sheriff's office porch. He turned to see Sheriff Young hang up the desk phone. Only now, when it was nearing two in the morning, did the sheriff show even a hint of exhaustion.

"Chief," he said. He stood and stretched his back. "You better get yourself to bed."

"I want to be here when you bring in those thugs who attacked that drifter," Emery replied.

"You won't be seeing that tonight." The sheriff turned to grab his coat. "Night, Boone!"

"Night, boss!" Boone called from the back.

"Why not?" Emery demanded as the sheriff stepped out into the warm night.

The sheriff raised an eyebrow.

"They haven't come back to the hotel," he said.

"Have you checked the Blue House?" Sheriff Young gave him a disgusted look and Emery pressed, "You only called?"

"Irene's been on the wrong side of the law, Chief, and paid the price. Now that she has two kids to look out for, she'd sell out her grandmother to keep from going back to jail. She'd tell me if Philip Cabot returned to his cabin. He hasn't."

"You have a lot of faith in the people of this town."

"No, I don't. I just know them very well." The sheriff sighed and rubbed his face. "Anyway, as to your fancy-pants city boys, I have no idea where they are, but I've put out word over the wire that they are persons of interest."

"They could be out of the state by now!" Emery protested.

"Could be, but I doubt it. Left their baggage in their rooms. Hundred dollar suit, one of them, Mark said. They'll be back, Chief, and the night clerk has my number." He stepped in and his enormous form loomed over Emery's. "Let me do my job, sailor. I don't take kindly to vigilantes in my town. Go home."

Emery's head was throbbing. He need aspirin, water, and rest more than he cared to admit. There was little he could do here and there was always the strong possibility that Philip and his friends would return to Norah's house. If Philip did, Emery would rather talk to him without Sheriff Young's oily presence.

"All right, Sheriff," he said and turned to go to the car.

"And Chief?" Young's sweet and sour tone made Emery grit his teeth, but he stopped at the car door and turned.

"Sheriff?"

Young was leaning again the porch post now, watching him.

"Don't leave town without letting me know."

Emery couldn't even pretend to answer that one. He wrenched the door open to his car and sped off without another word, leaving the sheriff alone in the darkness.

***

Emery's head was even worse when he arrived home. He slipped quietly through the back porch entrance, only to nearly trip over Fido. The dog yipped, though he went quiet on Emery's command. He was slipping through the living room to the staircase when a sound from the sofa brought to him to a halt. The shifting moonlight, struggling through intermittent cloud cover, now broke through and poured over the dim outline of Norah, sleeping on the sofa, her dark hair laying in a tangle halo around her face. She looked beautiful, even in repose, and he paused to contemplate her.

"Charles?"

The whisper came from the stairs. Emery turned sharply and winced, wishing he hadn't.

Captain Donovan stood half way up the staircase, his ruffled hair almost as wild as his eyes. His robe was hastily thrown over his pajamas and he carried a shotgun in one arm, broken open and ready for the shells he carried in his other hand.

"Did you hear him?" he asked.

Emery's headache was instantly forgotten. "What are you doing?" he demanded in a whisper.

In two strides, he was at the bottom of the staircase, looking up at the man. "Where are you going?"

Donovan didn't even look at him. He was staring outside. "Did you hear him?" he hissed, his eyes glassed over. "Did you hear him, Charles?"

As if on cue, a stiff breeze poured in from the lake through the open windows. Emery turned instinctively. Rustling curtains fluttered in the wind and through them, he could see the patterns of moonlight shifting as clouds scuttled by. Cold, damp air curled about him, making Emery shiver involuntarily. The dog shifted closer to him, but showed no undue alarm and Emery heard nothing.

"Captain," he said but Donovan waved the hand holding shells.

"He was calling," the captain breathed. "Calling for me, threatening me..."

"Just now?"

"You pulled up and the headlights... I think they startled him..."

"Give me the shotgun," Emery commanded.

Like a child, Donovan did. Emery slipped two shells into the shotgun and snapped the barrel shut.

The click was sharp enough to stir Norah. She sat up with a weary, "What is it?"

Emery snapped, "Wait here. There's someone outside."

"What?" Now she was fully awake.

"Stay here," Emery ordered, seeing again, in his mind's eye, the pistol cracking down on the drifter's head.

He strode outside, Fido trotting sharply at his heels.

Outside, the sky was clearing again and the landscape was bright enough to see and be seen. Emery stuck close to the shadows of the house and Fido sniffed at his heels. But though he prowled about the perimeter of the house and then the grounds, checked under the boats, and even in the shed and the car, he saw nothing and no one. Fido was calm and alert, his ears twitching with each snapping twig and he gave no indication that there was anyone out there.

Finally, head sore and stumbling with exhaustion, Emery turned and went back inside.

Norah was waiting at the porch door, one hand high keeping her robe closed, the other hand low holding a pistol. She looked at him inquiringly and seemed to see his head bandage for the first time.

"Was it...?" she asked, tearing her eyes from the bandage.

"I couldn't find anyone," he said and indicated the pistol in her hand. "I didn't know you had one."

She glanced at the pistol, then back at him, a hint of a smile on her face.

"There's a lot you don't know about me, Chief," she said.

He grinned and instantly the head pain flared up again. He winced and reached to grip his forehead. Norah grasped him by the arm and pulled him inside.

"Your head – oh, Charles, what happened?"

They entered the living room, where Captain Donovan nervously waited. He took the shotgun from Emery and placed it against the wall. Norah, one arm wrapped around Emery's waist, helped him to sit on the sofa. She sat next to him and immediately began to fuss with the bandages.

"I'm all right," Emery said. "The doctor patched me up and said I was fit for duty."

"Doctors," Norah snorted, her fingers light and cool against his skin. "Chief Emery, what *have* you been up to without me?"

"Did you see him?" Captain Donovan lowered his face until he was level with Emery's. His wide eyes and desperate tone made Emery want to shake him. "Did you see anyone?"

"There's no one out there," Emery said. His head weighed about fifty pounds and he was exhausted, almost too exhausted to talk. He should lie down. He should go to bed. But he was oddly reluctant to leave that sofa. "I looked, but there was no one."

"Who did this?" Norah demanded. She took Emery's chin and turned it towards her. "What happened, Emery?" Up close, her dark eyes were sparkling with concern and care, though her expression was firm.

"Tom Murphy tried to rob the diner tonight," he said and noticed that his mouth was dry. "I got in his way."

Her face softened. "Oh, Charles!"

Emery fought an almost overwhelming urge to pull her into his arms.

"Murphy?" Donovan sat on the coffee table, sagging with disappointment. "Poor Tom. Poor, poor Tom."

"What happened?" Norah asked.

"The sheriff interrupted him and Murphy ran into me while trying to escape. He's in jail now. Confessed to everything. Had to. He was caught with the lock box in his hand."

"Poor Tom," Donovan repeated.

"Everyone keeps saying that," Emery said sarcastically. "And yet I'm the one with the busted head."

"You need water and aspirin," Norah said and got up from the couch to fetch some. "And then you need to go to bed."

"I'll sleep down here," Emery said.

From the kitchen, she called back, "You will not! You will sleep in your bed and heal. I'll sleep down here with Fido and the pistol."

"Norah…"

"Charles." She reemerged with a glass of water and a bottle of pills and gave him a look of motherly firmness that should have irritated him. "I mean it. You need to rest. I have Fido and the pistol. And anyway, after so much excitement already tonight, what else do you think will happen?" She shook two pills into his hand and handed him the glass. "Swallow, drink, and then bed. That's an order, Chief."

He grinned up at her. "I'll sleep on the couch, ma'am."

She smiled and the smile touched her eyes. Then she turned to her father, who was still slumping silently on the table, lost in thought. "You too, Father."

"Yes, Norah," he said obediently.

But he did not move from his position on the table, not until Norah took the glass from Emery and went back into the kitchen. Then he moved close enough to touch Emery on the shoulder. When Emery looked up at him, his head aching bad enough to split in two, the eager look on Donovan's expression only made the older man look more unhinged.

"I heard him, Emery," he said in a whisper. "I heard him. He's waiting for me."

Exhaustion was rolling over Emery like a freight train. It was all he could do to keep from slumping over on the couch right then in there. With great effort, then, he reached up and patted Donovan on the hand.

"He'll have to get through me first," he said.

Donovan's eyes darted to the shotgun, then back to Emery. He looked relieved, but not overwhelmingly so, and he nodded.

"I'll have to face him one night, Emery," he said. "There's no way around it. I have to do it. I have to face it."

Emery was trying to keep his eyes open. "Not tonight, Captain," he said and lowered his voice as Norah reentered the room. "Not tonight."

Donovan nodded in understanding. When Norah again ordered him upstairs, he went without complaining. Emery stayed awake just long enough to see the pair of them disappear up the stairs and then blackness rolled over him and he knew no more that night.

18

It was the barking that he heard first, hysterical and deep, a frantic baying for help. Emery was deep in a dreamless sleep, so deep that he thought the sound was itself a dream. But the barking grew louder and then, over that, as Emery was rising from his dream slowly into consciousness, he heard the choking sound of a scream.

Norah's scream.

Instantly, he was awake. The room was shrouded in gray, with the new dawning sun struggling to cut through the cloud cover. Emery threw his legs over the couch and lunged for the shotgun. His vision churned like he was trying to stand on a deck in a storm. His legs snagged on a blanket he didn't remember pulling on last night.

Norah screamed again – this time, it was cut off.

Emery kicked off the blanket, grabbed the shells on the nearby table and slammed them into the barrel as he charged for the door. Donovan shouted, "Charles, what is it?" from behind him, but Emery didn't turn.

He burst through the door and turned a sharp left towards Fido's baying. There, a narrow path ran along the side of the lake, covered in pine needles and shaded with trees one side and bushes up against the lakeside. He ran, legs pumping, heart racing, the shotgun heavy in his arms. Now outside, he could see silver light battling the foggy gloom of the new day and hear the splashing sounds of a desperate struggle. Fido barked once more and then there was another splash. Norah shouted again, choking and coughing. Emery could see her and ran faster. Donovan shouted again, but he was far behind now.

Emery's foot caught on a projecting tree root and he nearly took a spill. Recovering his balance, he shouted, "Norah!"

A choking, sputtering sound nearby was the only reply. He ran a few more yards and the bushes broke and he suddenly found himself on a beach.

On his right, a meadow of reeds swayed violently. Fido's growl was low and terrifying. Emery charged into the water without thinking.

"NORAH!"

The water quickly became waist high. He tore through the reeds that snaked around his legs and obscured his vision. He heard Norah choking again and his fury grew. With a tremendous effort, he smashed through the last of the reeds and suddenly found himself in open water again.

Fur churned the water. Only a few feet away, Norah lay still, face down in the water.

Emery shouted and lunged now chest-deep into the water. He reached out and wrapped his arm around Norah's torso, pulling her up. Her head came up out of the water, dripping and motionless.

"Norah! Norah!"

He shook her and her head rolled back. She was white as a sheet.

Emery's heart stopped.

The churning suddenly grew less. Fido's head popped up and he barked. Then he started to swim, following the ripples of the underwater swimmer, who was heading back towards the house.

Donovan arrived on the shore just as Emery did. Emery barely heard his cries of anguish as he tossed the shotgun aside and pressed his fingers against her neck, desperately seeking a pulse. He put his ear against her chest, but there was nothing.

Norah, please... please...

Donovan was saying something, but Emery couldn't hear him. Without thinking, he began artificial respiration, trying not to think, trying not to picture this not working.

Norah, please... God, please, not her, not today...

As if in answer to his prayer, Norah began to choke up water. Her body convulsed with the effort, curling around like a child, her face turning red now. Emery went weak with relief. Almost before she was finished, he pulled her up off of the ground and into his arm. He held her, letting her shake and cough into his chest, feeling her heart beat against his chest. One of her hands curled, grabbing his shirt and holding him close, too.

Thank you, God, thank you, God...

He didn't realize he was saying this out loud,

his face buried in her wet hair until Donovan repeated, "Yes, yes, oh thank God!" He laid his hand on Emery's shoulder, reminding him of where he was and whose daughter he was cradling. Yet he probably would have held her longer had Fido's bark not reminded him of what had brought them out there to begin with.

Norah was still curled up against him, shaking and coughing, but Fido's bark was insistent. Emery gently untangled her hand from his shirt and pushed her into Donovan's arms. Then he grabbed the dripping shotgun and hopped up to run back towards the dock.

He arrived at the foot of Donovan's dock in time to hear two things: Fido's last bark, warning off the intruder, and the sound of a car engine, roaring to life on the road. He was just hesitating when he caught sight of the slim figure of a man, running with a curious limp down the driveway towards the road.

Emery's temper snapped.

"STOP!"

He charged towards the driveway, bringing the shotgun up and to bear on the runner, but the fog was still thick and the figure disappeared. Emery pushed himself, his legs pumping, adrenaline fueling his mad dash. He heard a door slam and the roar of the engine and pushed himself to run even faster.

The fog broke as he reached the bottom of the gravel driveway and the road beyond. The car was just rounding the bend in the road, spitting gravel as the driver pushed the engine. Without a second thought, Emery brought the shot gun up and fired. A blast of bird shot scattered and tore at the surrounding trees, but whether any hit the car, Emery couldn't tell. His fury and fear carried him several dozen feet down the road before it occurred to him that he couldn't possibly catch up with a motor car. But he could in his own car.

He did an abrupt about face and was just grabbing the door handle of his own car, when Fido came running into the drive, dripping wet and barking like mad. When he saw Emery, he barked again and turned, looking back at Emery as if to say, "Follow."

Emery did and they didn't stop until they were at the end of the dock. The lake spread out before them, shrouded in ghostly fog, the water only visible for a few feet. Fido barked into the fog and looked up at Emery, expectantly. But Emery could see nothing and heard far less.

"Who was it, boy?" he asked, as though the dog could answer.

Fido barked once more, then shook himself thoroughly, showering Emery with condensation. The threat, it seemed, had passed.

Emery turned back to the drive, and saw Norah, limping back into the yard on Donovan's arm. She was shaking, her arms pinned close to her side, and she leaned on her frail father for warmth.

Her robe and towel were on the dock beside Emery. He grabbed them and strode down the dock towards them, Fido trotting at his side.

Norah stepped out of her father's embrace to accept the towel. She looked frightened, her eyes huge in her face, and she let Emery drape the robe over her shoulders like she was a child.

"Thank you," she whispered.

"We heard a shot," Donovan said eagerly. "Did you see it?"

But Emery barely heard him. He was too busy staring at Norah's shoulder.

He'd been so concerned about her drowning that he hadn't noticed the injuries before. Seeing them now made heat pound in his temples. Norah's face was white and she shook under Emery's hand. The attacker had torn the bathing suit strap so that her bleeding shoulder was bare. There were scratches on her chin, shoulder, and legs, most bleeding, but all shallow. Barring infection, she would survive without a visible scar, but that was hardly the point. The sight of the blood angered Emery, but it was the fear in Norah's normally proud face that made him want to punch through something. It was all he could do not to pull the girl into his arms again.

She saw the anger and she pulled the robe on further, obscuring the wounds. "I'm all right," she said quietly. "Thanks to you and Fido."

"Who did this?" he managed, through gritted teeth. "Who attacked you?"

"It happened so fast. I was swimming – and something grabbed me. I kicked and fought, but the grip..."

She glanced down at her leg and Emery followed her gaze. Her ankle was ripped and reddened, something like a rope burn, where someone obviously tried to pull her under.

"Oh my God..."

Captain Donovan swayed like he was about to fall down. He turned and stumbled off to lower himself on one of the dock pilings. He looked frailer than he ever had.

Norah's voice was soft. "He was so strong..."

Emery jumped on that: "He?"

"I think so. I don't know. It's all a blur." She wrapped her arms around her waist and shivered. She attempted a smile, but she wouldn't look him in the eye. She was looking at his shirt. "I'm sorry – I got blood on you."

"Forget it."

She looked at him then, with dark enormous eyes and Emery's gut twisted.

He could have killed her.

A motor boat sped by the shore, casting white capped waves in their direction. Emery turned sharply, bring the shotgun up again. Fido ran to the water's edge and stood there, barking. But there was a change in his tone now – it was not so ferocious and Emery understood instantly. The drunken simpletons in the boat were not the ones that had attacked his mistress only a few moments ago. Almost as if on cue, Emery's battered head began to pound in earnest.

"Oh my God," Donovan said again. "Oh my God, Norah, I'm so sorry."

Norah shifted and some of her own frailty fell away. She became the caretaker again, even as Emery watched. "Father," she said, firmly. "This wasn't your fault."

"It was," the old man whispered. "It was."

She looked away from him to the shotgun in Emery's hands. "What did you see?"

It took Emery a second to answer. The sight of the boat had brought a question to mind. There was a man in the car and a man running away from the house, and the third in the water. There must be a rendezvous point somewhere further down the road...

"Charles?" Norah was shivering but her voice was steady. "What did you see?"

He brought his gaze back to her. "A man running from the house."

Her eyes widened. "From the *house*?"

"He was running from the front door. I ran after him, but he got away in a car. They must have... attacked you to distract us – to gain access inside."

"Oh my God!" Donovan exclaimed uselessly.

"Who was it?" Norah asked.

"I didn't see his face. All I saw was the car."

Her eyes narrowed. "Whose car?"

At his look, she nodded and stood straighter.

"I'll go change," she said and was turning towards the house before Emery could stop her.

"Wait, let me go through the house first, make sure no one is in there."

"Charles, you saw him run away and..." she started impatiently. But something in his expression must have stopped her, for she paused, then nodded. "I'll wait."

"Come on, dog," Emery growled to Fido.

His inspection of the house was brief, but thorough and Norah was right – there was no one in there. But he did discover what they were after.

Norah and Donovan were waiting for him on the back porch. Norah was shivering again, her teeth chattering. Her father was sitting beside her, his arm wrapped around her for warmth. When Emery reappeared, Norah stood up, eager.

"Well?"

"No one's inside," he said. "But someone has been in your room, Norah. They had taken apart a jewelry box."

"What?" Without waiting for permission, she ran inside, calling over her shoulder, "*Don't* leave without me, Emery. Without me, you won't know what was stolen!"

She had that right.

Emery turned to Donovan, who stood with his hands useless at his side, a look of puzzlement on his face.

"We were robbed?" he asked, helplessly.

"Yes. The place was ransacked."

Donovan turned away from him to the lake. One hand went up into his hair, an old gesture that spoke of being beyond his depth.

"But the monster couldn't have gone into the house," he whispered. "Or could he...?"

That snapped Emery out of his reverie and revived his ire. He strode forward and stood next to the man, trying to keep his temper, trying to remind himself that Donovan was old and didn't know what he was talking about.

"No, Captain," he said through gritted teeth. "He couldn't have done that. But I have a pretty good idea of who did. And I'm going to stop him."

Donovan's wide-eyed gaze looked childlike and for the first time, Emery wanted nothing so much as to shake the wonder out of his look.

"Who?" he whispered. "Who are you going to stop?"

"Donovan, knock it off."

Now he got angry. "Who, Emery?"

There was a moment of silence, then Emery said, "Your nephew. Philip."

"Philip?" Donovan's surprise was genuine. "But why?"

"He's in debt. He needs the money. So he took advantage of Norah's swim to gain access to the house."

"Oh." Donovan sounded subdued.

Emery, who'd been expecting an argument, was

surprised at the sudden silence. Both men turned back to the lake. Emery's mind whirled with possibilities. The gloom was shifting fast now and the fog hung low over the water. Already his field of vision was shortened and all he could see of the island was the hint of darkness in the mist.

He could have killed her. His own cousin. His grip on the shotgun tightened at the thought. He'd have to proceed carefully. His temper was only just barely contained and right now, even the memory of Philip's smug face was enough to make it snap to life again.

Donovan's sigh of relief broke through Emery's thoughts and brought him back into the present.

"Poor Philip," Donovan said. "He always did run with a bad crowd."

Emery's tempered flared. He swung about, his face hard. "Your poor nephew almost killed your daughter this morning!"

"You think *Philip* did that?"

"Either him or one of his buddies. He could have killed her, Captain, and I'm going to see to it that they all rot in jail."

"But Charles..."

"Captain, I know you don't want to hear this and I know this is painful. But your nephew has been conspiring to drive you off this property so he can bail himself out of debt with some city thugs. He's going to jail."

"But he'd never..."

"But he *did*. He hired a local bum to try to scare you while he was gone and when that didn't work, he came back to finish the job personally. And now..." he gritted his teeth and pounded his fist into his hands, "he's hurt Norah."

"He didn't do it!" The captain's voice was a roar now, echoing across the lake. "He *didn't* attack Norah, Charles! He'd never hurt her!"

"Someone did, Captain," Emery matched his tone. "Someone just did!"

"I know!" Captain Donovan's eyes were wide now, angry, but he was holding his ground. "It *wasn't* Philip. It was the creature. I *heard* him, Emery. I heard him, calling out to me from across the water, taunting me, drowning her to get to me!"

It was as if all of the air had been sucked out of Emery's lungs. He gaped at the raging old man, red-faced and eyes wild, fists clenched in sudden vicious, helpless anger. This was not the man that Emery had known – this was a stranger, and suddenly, what Philip Cabot and Sheriff Young claimed appeared all too true.

"Captain," he said slowly. "What are you telling me?"

"Are you blind?" Donovan hissed. He stepped closer, and suddenly it was Emery taking a defensive step back. "It wasn't Philip – it couldn't have been. Look at those cuts, man. It wasn't a man, it was that *thing,* out there. It grabbed her thinking she was me. It's that monster, Charles, and he's not going to stop until he finishes the job. Until he gets me or I get him." His crazed gaze shifted to the gray, shrouded water over Charles' shoulder. "Tonight. We've got to kill it tonight. We've got to kill it or else…"

There was ice in Charles's veins now. He stared at Donovan, hoping that the dawning horror in his heart wasn't visible in his face.

He has *gone mad,* he thought. *It's over.*

"Captain," he said quietly. "We have proof. I found the bum. He half-way confessed before passing out. It isn't a creature. It's very human and very dangerous."

"You aren't listening to me!" Donovan cried. He stormed over to the water's edge and pointed out into the fog and gloom. "That creature's out there, *now*, and he's coming for me. He's coming for us. He'll wait for dark – he always waits for dark – but we have to stop him, Emery! Before someone else gets hurt."

Emery stepped forward. "There is no creature, Captain," he said. "There never was a creature. He was always and ever was a coping mechanism for you to handle Jasper Smith's death."

Donovan staggered as though struck. "Emery," he whispered. "What are you telling me?"

You're insane. You're dangerous. And I may not be able to protect you from yourself or anyone else.

But Emery didn't say any of those things. He took a deep breath and another step forward until now he close enough to the old man to lower his voice so that the words didn't carry. He didn't shout, but then he didn't have to. Every word was like a blow from a heavy baseball bat and each swing made contact.

"You asked me to find out the truth, Captain. You told me whatever it was, you'd accept it from me. Do you still intend to stand by that?"

Donovan's eyes were enormous. He stood as though bracing himself against an attack.

"I'll accept whatever the truth is," he said.

Emery nodded and drew in a breath. "That night on the boat, you were both drunk and careless. Jasper fell overboard. It was an accident. You were unable to save him and your guilt created a creature you could blame. There never was a sea satyr. He was invented to save you from a lifetime of guilt."

Donovan was still now, still as death itself. Emery pushed himself to finish, to make sure the old man *heard*. "There was only ever a tragic accident at sea and a greedy nephew who wanted to set his ailing uncle up in the loony bin. It's *over*, Captain Donovan. Let me finish it now. Let me protect you."

Before his eyes, Donovan withered away in the skeleton of a drunken old fool that he'd been when Emery first arrived.

"You don't believe me," he whispered. "You never believed me."

Emery tried to moderate his tone, but there was nothing that could make what he had to say easier to hear. "Captain, I never believed in fairy tales. The creature was never really an option."

It was finished. He turned and stalked towards the driveway. Norah reappeared on the porch, dressed in a soft woolen dress and carrying what looked to be a bundle of clothes with her.

"I have a list of the stolen items," she said. "Are we going to the police?"

For a brief second, Emery thought about leaving her behind. But he still didn't know where Philip was and the idea of leaving her seemed untenable.

"We'll all go together." He turned to Donovan. "Captain!"

The captain was standing, slump-shouldered at the end of the dock. He barely turned his head in their direction. Fido remained at his side, looking up at his master.

"Come with us," Emery said.

There was a pause, then Donovan shook his head.

"I want to think," he said. "I'll stay here."

A thought crossed Emery's mind. He handed Norah the shotgun and trotted back down the dock to the old man. Donovan didn't raise his head when Emery said, "You won't do anything foolish while I'm gone? You'll still be here when we come back?"

There was a beat, then Donovan looked up at him.

"If you're worried about me killing myself," he said softly. "I'd never do that to Norah." Some life flashed back into his eyes, a momentary revival. "Protecting her was the only reason I brought you here, Emery. And I'll ensure her happiness and safety if it's the last thing I do."

Suddenly Emery became aware of a wall, thick and impenetrable, coming up between him and his one-time mentor. Donovan had stepped away from him, as he'd stepped away from everyone else, isolating himself as he had done before Emery came. The loss was swift and more painful than Emery was prepared for. But it was hardly unexpected – hadn't Emery just told him he was crazy?

"We'll be back as soon as possible," Emery said. "Stay here."

Donovan reached down to ruffle Fido's head. "We'll be here."

Emery didn't trust him, but a sudden rush of anxiety – to catch Philip, to stop the cruel campaign and salvage what little sanity remained in the tortured old man – made him turn on his heel and hurry down the dock. Norah was waiting for him, watching the little drama with a puzzled expression. Emery took her arm and started her towards the car.

"What happened?" she asked.

"The captain is going to stay here, look after the place."

"Oh!" She grasped the implications with lightning speed. "Is he... okay?"

"He'll be fine. He needs some space."

She nodded, relieved. "All right. And Emery... I think I know where he would have gone with that stuff. But we'll have to hurry. And here." She shoved the bundle of blankets into his arms. "I'll drive. You change. You look like you've been in two fights."

They were at the car now and Norah grabbed the driver's side door before he could protest. He looked down at his clothes. He was still wearing the same outfit from yesterday, having been too tired to change when he arrived last night. Now they were wet and bloody from his adventure in the water, and stained with dirt and dried blood from his tussle in the alley.

"You think of everything," he said.

She grinned. "Just get in. We have a felon to catch."

Part 3: The Showdown

19

Somewhat awkwardly, Emery changed in the back seat while Norah drove. She was a fair driver, hugging the corners and turns, and picking up speed on the straight roads. It wasn't until Emery had finished dressing and climbed into the front passenger seat that he realized they weren't heading for town.

"I thought we were headed for the police station?" he said.

She shook her head, her eyes fixed on the road. "It'll take too long to convince Young."

"That there was a break-in?"

"I want to stop him, Charles. He took my mother's engagement ring and locket. It's…" Her voice waivered, and then strengthened with resolution. "I won't wait for Young."

Emery didn't protest. "So where are we going?"

"There's a pawn shop in Rochester. The owner is a school friend of Philip's. He doesn't ask questions and he's always available when Philip needs a hand. Don't ask me how I know."

"I won't."

She shot him a sly look. "I listened in on one of his telephone calls."

"Miss Donovan, you should be a detective."

The humor faded from her expression. "Some detective. You've discovered more in three days than I have in my entire life."

Emery watched as she deftly maneuvered around a slow-moving tractor and shifted gears. Her face tightened, her knuckles grew white with increased pressure. She was starting to recover from the incident earlier this morning and, as her fear and shock faded, the next set of reactions were beginning to appear. Emery had seen this sort of thing before, on ships and on shore, in a variety of settings and with a variety of people, but never, he realized, with a woman.

He answered carefully: "I just know what questions to ask."

"Oh really?" she snapped. "You knew what questions to ask my father? You knew how to ask about Jasper's accident and about the asylum and his nightmares – how remarkable!" She slammed into another gear. "For your information, Emery, I asked those questions too, both at the time and later. Unfortunately for me, my parents' answers were more fiction than fact. And now that fiction results in *this*: my house being broken into. My terrified father being driven back to the asylum because my worthless cousin can't stop gambling!" She slammed the dashboard with her palm. "*Why didn't they tell me*? I'm their *child*. Their only child now! I had a right to know!"

He waited a beat before responding: "Why?"

She looked at him in shock, the movement so sudden that she unconsciously jerked the wheel in the same direction. "Why?"

"What right had you to know? You *are* their child. They are your parents. They have the right to protect you."

"Protect me? From what? Embarrassment? I don't care about that! I care about them!"

"That is self-evident," he said.

"Then what?" she demanded hotly. "If you know everything, tell me now. Why wouldn't they tell me?"

"Because you would care," he said.

"Chief Charles Emery, you are the most aggravating...!"

"You know now," he interrupted. "Your father lost his friend at sea and suffered a mental collapse that earned him a stay in a looney bin. How does that make you feel?"

"Angry. I should have been told."

"Beyond the anger. What do you feel?"

Norah took a deep breath and flexed her fingers on the steering wheel. Her posture softened as she admitted, "Sad. Scared. Protective."

He jabbed a finger at her. "Bingo."

Her brow creased. "What are you saying?"

"I'm saying that they were adults when this happened."

"So was I!"

"You were an adult," he agreed calmly. "A woman with a career and a life in Boston. A woman who they thought was going to get married. A woman who then gave up all of those things to move north to look after her parents when her mother became ill. A woman who, I would guess, didn't think twice about doing so, because she has a keen sense of obligation to the people that raised her and knew that, with her brother's loss, she was their only living relative. They didn't tell you, Norah, because they loved you enough to want you to have a life of your own. They are good parents. And you should honor that."

They drove in silence for a long time. Emery turned to look out his window, to give Norah time to process what he'd said. Miles of trees and fields whirled by unseen as he thought through his statement over and over, wondering if he'd said too much or too little or if he should have said anything at all.

Do all women make you second guess things? he wondered. *Or just this woman?*

Finally, it was Norah who broke the silence.

"I guess..." she said and trailed off.

Emery looked at her. Her profile was thoughtful, her posture relaxed, and her eyes were firmly focused on the road. He waited.

"I guess," she said again slowly, "sometimes it

takes an outsider to see what's really happening in a situation."

He *really* didn't like the term 'outsider', but all he said was, "Sometimes problems are too close to see clearly." After a moment, he added, "Your father knows me pretty well. He knew that I'm not sentimental – I wouldn't be swayed by affection."

Now she gave him a sidelong look with just a hint of amusement.

"Not even a little?" she asked.

Emery just grinned back and then they both turned back to the road.

****

It took them about an hour to get into Rochester. From what little Norah said, Emery gathered that this was better travel time than average, but as there were no police cars to be seen, he didn't mind so much. His head was starting to hurt again and every time he looked at Norah, her hair still damp, all he could see was her body laying still in the water and his heart would clench tight. He had a score to settle – breaking a minor law seemed a fair trade to stop a greater evil.

Rochester was a typical rambling New Hampshire mill city. The outer layer of small family farms gave way to broad streets flanked by brick buildings or over-sized Victorian houses that now boasted of rooms for let. The mills themselves were still in operation, though many doubted they would survive the decade. Despite this, it was a pretty city that had made a visible effort to keep up appearances. Emery was pleased to see that civic pride had not completely gone to the wayside.

Norah said, as she turned the car down Laramie Street, "We're almost there and now I'm wondering: if Philip gave the goons his car, how will he...?"

"Get there?" Emery shrugged. "The New York boys have a vested interest in getting Philip to the pawn shop, don't worry."

"I just hope we arrive before they leave."

"They had to pick up the swimmer, which I think will even out our time."

"Swimmer?" He gave her a look and she unconsciously ran her hand through her hair. "Oh," she said softly. "I'd almost forgotten."

"I haven't. And I won't any time soon either."

They were in a quieter, more rundown part of the city. Apartment buildings and tenements sat silently on either side, with only the occasional elderly person or mother with a baby carriage walking the streets. Children were in school, most parents were at work, and there was so little here to steal that cops weren't to be expected on the streets. Emery's car got maybe one glance of interest, but that was all.

Emery opened the glove compartment. Norah's eyes widened when he pulled out the revolver. He checked it, spun the cylinder to check the cartridges, and then slipped it into his waistband. Her eyes were still on him when he looked up.

"I was in such a hurry, I'd forgotten to bring a weapon," she said sheepishly. "I should have known you wouldn't make the same mistake."

"No, ma'am," he said. "I'll make different mistakes, but not that one. How far are we from the shop?"

"It's down the next street."

"Then pull over here. I don't want to be seen."

She drove a little further, then pulled into an alley and killed the engine.

"The shop is right in front of us," she said and then brightened. "We aren't too late, look!"

She pointed. Emery had to lean closer to her to see. Across the street, a dirty sign announced "Faraday Street Pawn Shop" while an arrow indicated a basement shop space. To the right was an alley and parked in the shadows was a familiar looking car. As Emery watched, he saw something shift in the shadows.

Evidentially, Norah did not see it, for she had just opened her door and was moving quickly to leave. Emery acted quicker. He leaned across and yanked the door shut again, ignoring her squawk of protest.

"We have to stop them!" she said. "Emery, they are in there now, all of them!"

"Not all of them," he replied.

As if on cue, a tiny flame burst to life in the shadow of the alley. It rose to light a cigarette and briefly illuminate Alph's strong-jawed face. The match went out, but the glowing end of the cigarette remained and Norah sank back into her seat, pale.

"I would have walked right into him," she whispered.

"He wouldn't have known how to handle you," he said lightly and she snorted in amusement.

"Okay then," she said, with an attempt at courage. "Now what?"

Emery kept his eyes on the street. "What was your plan?"

"Plan? What plan?"

"You wanted to come straight here without consulting the police."

"I want to stop Philip from selling my mother's jewelry, which they are doing right now. We should stop them, Charles!"

"Do you really think Alph and Vinny are just going to let him give them back to you?"

She opened her mouth, then closed it again. "You let me drive all the way here..." she started, accusingly, and he had to nod in acceptance.

"I lost my temper," he admitted. "I wasn't thinking clearly."

She flushed and looked back at the shop. "Neither was I, I guess. So... what do we do?"

"I don't care about the goons," he said, even though a part of him did very much care about the goons. "I do care about Philip. And I'll get your jewelry back."

"You expect me to just let you handle this?"

"I'm asking you to let me handle this," he corrected. "I'm also asking you to drive to the nearest police station – or pay phone – and get them to come to the pawn shop. I'll keep Philip here."

"You'll need help."

"That's why I want you to bring the police."

"Emery, this is my family, my problem."

"It's my problem, too."

"Oh? And how do you figure that?"

He gave her another look. "Your father made it my problem. When they attacked you today... That made it personal."

Norah's mouth formed a little o. She caught herself and looked at the floor. "It was personal to me as well," she said. "I don't... This morning... Look, I know this isn't the best time, but it felt... I thought..." She drew a long breath and looked at him. "Philip isn't the only one at fault here. I don't want to let any of them get away. Not after what they did to me. Especially not after what they did to my father. I want them all, do you understand?"

Her eyes were fierce and shining. Emery nodded slowly.

"I'll keep them here," he said.

She drew in a breath. "I'll get the police."

"I'll leave you the shotgun."

"But..."

"It's too unwieldy."

He gave her a small smile, and then reached for the door handle. He stopped when her hand gripped his arm. He turned to see her giving him a stern look.

"You'll be safe?" she asked.

"No," he said. "But I'll be all right."

She smiled. "I guess that will have to do."

20

Emery stood in the darkness of the alleyway and waited until Norah had gone. The moment the car disappeared around the corner of the street, he began to move. He turned into Laramie Street and ran down a block. Then he took a left into an alleyway and stopped just short of Faraday Street.

Peering out, he saw that he was south of Alph's alleyway, just as he'd intended. From his position, he couldn't see Alph or the car, so he crossed the street and went north towards the pawn shop. Faraday Street was mostly residential and poorer than Laramie, with a few shops and pubs here and there to break things up. There were only a few people out here too. A woman smoked in the window of her tenement. A lethargic man cleaned the window of a ratty pub. Emery wasn't sure if this was to his advantage or not, but the memory of Captain Donovan's terrified expression and Norah's limp body sent ice through his veins and dashed all other considerations aside.

He came up to the alleyway and slowed, listening. Over the natural soundtrack of city noises, he heard the gentle squeak of a stiff leather shoe and low humming. Alph was still there.

Shielding his actions from the street with his body, Emery pulled his pistol out and held it low against his leg. Pressing himself close to the brick wall, he slowly angled his head until he could see into the alleyway.

The car was enormous, dwarfing the area. Just beyond its hulk, Emery saw Alph's broad-shouldered outline. The thug was leaning against the passenger door, hat cocked at an angle and cigarette burning low in his hand. He was looking dreamily northwards, into Faraday Street. His posture was deceptively peaceful – the humming was tuneless. He was a relaxed tiger, ready to spring at a moment's notice. But his back *was* to Emery.

Emery slipped into the alley and dropped low, keeping the car between him and the thug. He crept along the length of the car, keep his ear tuned into Alph's humming. He froze when the big thug shifted against the car. Between the wheels, Emery saw the glowing cigarette fall into the dirt. Alph's foot lifted and fell, rubbing the ember out as the humming took on an actual tune.

"Pack up all my cares and woe…" Alph sang low, almost happily. He shifted again before resuming his original position. "Here I go, singing low…" The humming and singing briefly stopped and the reason became clear when he sighed and smacked his lips after a long pull from a flask. "Bye, bye, blackbird."

Emery breathed in relief and continued moving forward. He rounded the back of the car and paused at the edge, waiting. Alph continued to sing badly, occasionally pulling from his flask and leaning against the car. Emery waited, feeling the sweat trickle down his side, knowing that if he waited too long, Vinnie and Philip would join him and his slight advantage would be lost.

When Alph's song ceased for another drink, Emery shoved himself upward, bringing the gun to bear on his opponent. The flask was still at

Alph's lips when Emery's cool voice cut through the peaceful stillness.

"Don't move. Keep your hands where I can see them."

He pulled the hammer back for extra emphasis.

Alph froze as commanded, his body stiffening.

Emery kept his voice low. "Drop the flask and turn – slowly."

The metal flask fell with a clink and the big man turned slowly, keeping his hands high above his head. His chiseled face looked hard and angry.

"Now, moving *very* slowly and *very* carefully, take your piece out and drop it to the ground." When Alph moved, Emery hissed, "Carefully, friend, carefully."

The thug growled, but the automatic dropped to the ground without any other protest. Emery nodded and stepped backwards, indicating with his pistol. "Come."

Alph followed until they were flush with the back of the car. Emery indicated the trunk of the car. "Open it."

The trunk door made a squeaking noise as Alph

lifted it. Emery swung the pistol. Alph crumbled to the ground without a sound.

Emery slipped the pistol back into his waistband and did a quick pat-down. Alph had a knife in his back pocket and a small pistol in an ankle holster. He pulled these out and then, with a good deal of effort, managed to get Alph's heavy body into the trunk of the car. He had hardly finished doing this when he heard steps sounding at the far end of the alley. He dropped the door and crouched down, pulling out his pistol again.

"Alph!"

Vinnie rounded the corner, his every movement announcing disgust and annoyance. He stopped just within the shadow of the alley and put his hands on his hips, looking around.

"Alph, get over here!"

Philip appeared behind him, but it was a very different man than the one that Emery had met just the other day. The swagger was long gone and in its place was a creeping, submissive, frightened man whose hunched shoulders belied his height. He was carrying an envelope in one hand and the other gingerly touched a blossoming bruise along his jaw.

He stopped at the entry of the alley and held out the envelope.

"Maybe we can work something out, Vin," he said.

With a vicious snarl, Vinnie turned on him. In a flash, Philip was pinned up against the wall, his head bouncing off the brick. His captor pressed him against the wall with one arm while his other hand drew his pistol and pressed it up under Philip's chin.

"We ain't working nothing out," he hissed. "The grace period has ended and you didn't pay."

"It's not my fault! I didn't know the jewelry was so worthless – what do I know about that? Take the envelope and give me more time!"

"You just don't get it, do you, Cabot?" he snarled and pressed harder, forcing Philip's head up. "We aren't the local bank. You don't get credit because you *tried* hard."

Philip whimpered. "Give me more time! I need more time. My uncle, I can…"

"You've had all the time you're going to get,

Cabot. My boss is not a patient man." Vinnie shifted his stance and his foot hit Alph's abandoned gun, sending it skittering across the hard-packed dirt. Vinnie glanced down and instantly recognized the significance. In a well-practiced move, he wrenched Philip away from the wall and turned him into a human shield, one arm pinning him by the neck while the other pressed the pistol to his temple.

"Come out or I'll kill him!"

Philip's whimper filled the empty air.

Emery rose to his feet and brought his revolver to bear on the pair of them. "Drop it, Vinnie."

Vinnie's head snapped in his direction and before Emery could fire, he'd turned to position Philip between them. Only then did the thug's expression turn to surprise, then curiosity.

"You're like a bad penny," he said. "Where's Alph?"

"He's out of the picture," Emery said. "Let Cabot go."

"Oh, no, Chief. Phil and me have become inseparable since you saw us last, isn't that right, Phil?"

"Please, Vinnie," Philip whimpered, but Vinnie's grip only tightened.

"This is a private affair, Emery," Vinnie said grimly. "I'm willing to overlook your interference if you step away now."

Emery shook his head. "Sorry, that's not how this works."

"What are you, a Fed?"

"Shall we say a concerned citizen?"

Vinnie grinned. "Did no one ever tell you that curiosity killed the cat?" He pushed the pistol into Philip's temple, making Philip crane his head. "Drop it, or pretty boy gets it."

"Kill the goose that has yet to lay the golden egg? I doubt your boss would like that."

"There are other ways for Philip to make good on his debt," Vinnie said. He nodded to the car and Philip closed his eyes as though in pain.

Emery's temper flared hot. He snapped, "You could have given them the *car* and yet you still went after the Captain?"

Philip's eyes flew open again and he snapped, "That land is *mine!* He's been living on it for *years* rent-free – I only wanted what was mine."

"A fascinating family drama," Vinnie said drily. "I guess you could say that we all want what's due us, eh, Chief?" He tightened his grip on Philip and the smaller man gave a choking cough. "Drop the piece and we all walk away with stories for our grandchildren."

Philip drew in his breath in a low hiss, his eyes closed as though in prayer. "Come on, Chief, just do as they ask."

Emery shook his head.

"You both lost your right to negotiate when you attacked Norah Donovan this morning."

The confused look on both of their faces very nearly threw him.

"Norah – attacked?" Philip gasped and then choked again when Vinnie jerked his arm.

"Enough! Drop it, Emery, or he dies!"

Emery hesitated.

Then, as if on cue, a siren ripped through the air. Vinnie jerked in surprise, his head whipping around. Emery fired. Philip screamed and dropped when Vinnie released him. Vinnie fired two shots at Emery before turning and fleeing. Something slammed into Emery's shoulder, almost costing him his grip on the pistol, but he ignored it and ran off in pursuit. He leapt lightly over Philip, who was writhing on the ground, clutching his bleeding arm, and emerged into the daylight-drenched street.

Vinnie was surprisingly fast for a man of his size – he was already a block away, his suit flapping in the breeze. Emery stopped and leveled his gun. Just as he squeezed the trigger, a police car cut into the street, its light flashing. Vinnie jerked when he heard the shot, turned, fired off one in return, and then tore down another alley.

The police car screeched to a halt and the cop inside was shouting, but Emery didn't hear him. He turned back into the alley and ran, passing Philip, who'd pushed himself up against the wall by this point. Emery ran, headache forgotten, shoulder pain pushed into the background. The only thing that mattered was catching Vinnie, stopping Vinnie. His legs pounded gravel and suddenly he was out in the sunshine of the next street. Vinnie was there, too, a black coated figure walking quickly down the sidewalk.

Emery didn't bother shouting. He ran, leather

slapping pavement, gun growing heavier and heavier in his hand. This street was busier – there were people out and about, some loitering, others walking purposefully, all of them turning to stare as he ran past. Something must have alerted his quarry, because Vinnie half turned. His gun came up and barked. People screamed. Emery ran on. Vinnie turned and ran. He was taller than Emery and theoretically should have been faster.

He wasn't. Emery closed the distance, so close that when Vinnie turned again, Emery was practically on top of him. Emery grabbed at Vinnie's gun arm. Vinnie turned, using Emery's own grip to throw him. Emery tripped and hit the pavement with his shoulder. Pain exploded, almost obscuring his vision and, but he turned the fall into a roll and came up with his pistol in hand. Vinnie fired, but his shot went wild. Emery's did not.

Vinnie gasped and went down, revealing the police car driving up. It barely stopped before a big, burly cop in a blue jacket hopped out, gun already in hand.

"Freeze, both of you!" he screamed.

Vinnie was down on one knee, one hand trying

to stop his leg from bleeding, the other already raising at the policeman's command. The cop charged over and kicked Vinnie's gun away before turning to Emery.

"Drop it, sunshine," he said. "Hands on your head."

Suddenly the gun was too heavy for Emery to hold. He obeyed and sagged.

The driver's door opened and the second cop came out, already fishing for handcuffs. Emery was saying, "There's another man – in the alleyway," when the back passenger door opened and Norah popped out. She ran to Emery, ignoring the cop's admonitions, her face white.

"Charles! You're hurt!"

It was only then that Emery thought to look at his shoulder. And it was only when he saw the blood, pooling out onto his jacket, that he realized that he had been shot.

21

Emery, Philip, and Vinnie were taken to be treated at the hospital on Charles Street while Alph was thought well enough to be taken right to the police station. Norah insisted on going to the hospital as well and drove herself.

At the hospital, the three men were separated and kept in secured rooms, while Norah remained in the waiting room, fending off reporters and answering police questions. In between treatments, all of the men were questioned thoroughly. The policeman taking Emery's statement looked doubtful as he made notes.

"This is far-fetched," he said. "Gangsters trying to turn an old man crazy so they can steal his land?"

"Technically, it's not his land," Emery said. "Talk to Miss Donovan – she knows those details."

"She's giving evidence now. How long have you known Miss Donovan?"

"About three days."

The policeman looked surprised, but only made a note. "You never met her before?"

"No. I knew her father years ago. I've been at sea. I'm a Navy man."

"You won't mind if I call the base to verify your identity?"

"I'd be insulted if you didn't. Oh, and you might call Sheriff Young of Deep Water and Doctor Otis Skinner in Holloway."

"Doctor Skinner?"

"He can confirm that both Cabot and I called making inquiries about Captain Donovan and his mental state."

The officer made another note then stood and said, "Doctor says you'll be fine to leave before the end of the day."

Emery nodded. "The bullet passed right through."

"You're lucky."

"I know. How is Cabot?"

"We'll know soon enough, though from the amount of complaining he's doing, you'd think he'd been riddle with dozens of shots. I have to tell you, Mr. Emery-"

"Chief."

"Chief, then. This is my town and we've been civilized for a long time. I don't like strangers coming here to work out their differences in a street battle. You want a showdown, you take it to Dodge City next time, you hear?"

Emery nodded. "I understand. What am I going to be charged with?"

"I'm still working that out."

"And Miss Donovan?"

The officer paused at the door, a slow smile crossing his face. "She's smart enough to call us and stay out of gun battles. She's only asking for you. I kept thinking you were the relative rather than Cabot."

"We've become close."

"In three days. Sure."

The officer left, leaving Emery to his thoughts.

***

It took nearly the rest of the day to sort everything out. Sheriff Young ended up driving into Rochester and after hours of negotiations that Emery knew nothing about, thanks to his being forced to stay in the hospital for the duration, managed to secure Norah and Emery's release, on the understanding that they weren't to leave the state without notice. Young seemed quite proud of this concession, though he made it clear that he thought this whole incident a waste of his precious time.

"I don't care for vigilantes, Chief," he said as he waited for the nurses to finish rewrapping Emery's shoulder. "Next time you think there's a problem, call us in, will you?"

"What do you think Norah was doing?" Emery asked, testily. His adrenaline had long worn off and the wound, though uncomplicated and clean, was painful. His headache was back too and he wasn't in the mood for Young's sarcasm. "Where is she, by the way?"

"Down by the car. She insisted on driving you home. Said it was the least she could do under the circumstances." He added, as a sort of afterthought, "She is a good woman."

Emery didn't respond to that. "What about Cabot?"

"The locals are holding him and I gather that's fine by Philip. The people he's mixed up with won't take too kindly to his getting Vinnie and Alph locked up."

"They'll be coming for him."

"Probably."

"Sheriff..."

"Which is why I suggested, rather strongly, that he take the bull by the horns and sell that damned car. Can't think of why he didn't do it in the first place."

"Will it cover the debt?"

"How should I know? It's a show of good faith, if nothing else."

The nurse finished with him and offered to help him out of the hospital. Young declined for him and they waited in silence until she gathered her supplies and left. Then Emery said, "Sheriff, if

Captain Donovan finds out about this, he'll allow Philip to sell his house to keep him from getting killed."

"I reckon you're right." Young nodded lazily. "Families do that for one another."

"Frankly Cabot doesn't deserve to get out of it, after what he tried to pull."

"You think the mob ought to have him?"

"Don't put words in my mouth," Emery snapped. "Cabot and his cronies attacked Norah today and nearly drowned her."

"Norah mentioned that."

"And?"

"And they denied it. All three of them. Categorically. If I didn't know better, I'd have believed them, too."

"They're lying. I'll bet he lied about trying to run Captain Donovan off as well."

"Nope. Coughed up to that one. Frankly, Cabot is so desperate for our protection that he confessed to almost everything. Said he learned the captain had a fear of sea creatures after a drinking bout with him one night, so he hired the hobo to mark up the boat and throw a scare into the old man to drive him off of the property."

"It nearly worked, too."

"I'll say. He didn't mean to cause the heart attack, although he wasn't above using it to his advantage."

"Swine. He did attack Norah - she'd be dead if I hadn't found her."

"But you did. I don't know why he's holding out on that charge, but give us some time to persuade him to tell the truth. On occasion, we are rather good at it." He jerked his head towards the door. "Come on. Miss Donovan is waiting for you."

Norah was by the car. The careworn look on her face melted away to a bright, relieved smile when she saw him. Rather than run to him, like Emery rather hoped she would, she went around and opened the passenger door for him.

Young waited until they were settled in, then he leaned on the door and looked down into Norah's window.

"You drive safe, now," he said. "And tell your father I hope he's well."

"I will, Sheriff," she said. "And thank you."

He smiled at her – a genuine smile this time. "It was a pleasure. Just try to stay out of trouble, will you?"

She shot Emery a look. "I'll do my best, but no promises."

Sheriff Young stepped back from the car and she put it into gear and drove off. Her driving was much smoother now and Emery commented, "You're getting the hang of this thing."

"Looks like I'd better, what with you getting shot up and all," she said lightly. Then she sobered. "Are you in pain?"

"The doctor put me on so much medication, it's a wonder I can feel my toes."

She laughed. "I don't really believe that, but I'll pretend I do."

Her eyes were shining, and after a moment, Emery straightened up in his seat.

"I'm all right, Norah, really."

"I know and... well, thank God because I..." She wiped her eyes roughly with her palm. "God, Emery, I didn't know it was going to turn out like that."

"None of us did," he said ruefully. "But no one got hurt."

She raised an eyebrow, so he amended, "Badly."

"Well, I'm glad," she declared firmly. "Because I wouldn't want to have to explain to the Navy how I cost them one of their own."

"One of their best."

"Oh, is that right?"

He shrugged. "Modesty compels me to be truthful. You believe me?"

"I'll pretend I do."

"My ego thanks you."

"Any chance you're hungry? Because suddenly I'm starving."

"I could eat a horse."

"You may end up doing that," she said, as she turned to park in front of a worn-out looking diner. "This reminds me, I want to call Father. I didn't have a chance to in the hospital and he'll be worried sick by this time."

Or dead drunk, Emery thought, but for Norah's sake, he didn't say it out loud.

***

The diner was a modest establishment that watered their beer and over-cooked their cheap beef, but Emery was too hungry to be particular and Norah was too preoccupied to mention anything. There was a pay phone and she tried the house three times, once before their meal and then twice while Emery was paying the tab. When Captain Donovan didn't pick up the phone the first time, she said, "He's probably out on the lake." When he didn't pick up the second time, she told Emery that perhaps he hadn't heard the ring.

Between the food, the beer, and the time spent relaxing in the booth, Emery was starting to tire and ache. His shoulder, which had only marginally bothered him earlier, was beginning to really hurt now, especially when he had to adjust the sling to reach his wallet. Even as he walked to the phone booth, he found himself wishing he were back in Donovan's lake house, in the pale blue guest room under the covers.

One look at Norah's face as she sat in the phone booth, waiting for Donovan to pick up this third time and Emery knew that the day was far from over. She looked up at him, her pale face pinched with worry.

"He's not answering, Charles," she said in a hoarse voice that was almost a whisper. "Where could he be?"

"He could be outside," Emery replied and nodded to the window. The late afternoon sun was shafting deep into the near-deserted dining room. "It's a nice afternoon. Maybe he went fishing. Or took Fido for a walk."

"I guess he could be at the neighbor's," she said reluctantly. But she didn't move and she didn't hang up and the tinny, faraway sound of the phone ringing through the speaker kept going on and on.

"Isn't it possible?"

"It's possible."

"But...?"

"I don't know. I just... I have a bad feeling, Emery. I really do. Something's wrong." She hung up suddenly, as though annoyed. "Something's bad."

Emery's exhaustion was threatening to peak. He wanted to say, "You're tired, you've been scared, you're just imagining things," because that was what he believed. But looking at her now, he knew that saying any of that would be a mistake. So he said instead, "Why don't you call the Jensens?"

Her face brightened and she did.

She explained the break-in that morning to Mrs. Jensen and made her concerns appear limited to her father's state of mind. Mrs. Jensen was, of course, very excited to hear about the break-in and relieved that the thieves were caught. She reported that her husband hadn't yet come home from work, but she expected him shortly.

"I'll send one of the boys over to check on your father," she said. "Don't you worry none. I expect he's out fishing or just fallen asleep or something."

"Thank you, Mrs. Jensen, I sure appreciate it."

"No trouble at all. What are neighbors for, after all?"

Norah hung up the phone and looked away from Emery for a moment, drumming her fingers on the phone book. Finally, she looked up at him and admitted, "I must be tired or something. But I can't shake the feeling that something really is wrong."

"Well, then let's go home and find out."

He held out a hand to her. She took it and,

after he'd pulled her to her feet, she squeezed it gratefully.

"Let's go home," she said.

22

Emery still couldn't drive, so it was Norah that took the wheel. About a half an hour from Deep Water, the tire gave out, forcing Norah to the side of the road and Emery to wake from his drowsing stupor. Norah managed to pull the car to a halt safely and they sat for a moment in silence, catching their breath. Then she slammed the steering wheel with both palms.

"The sun will be down before we get home!" she said and slammed her way out of the car before Emery could respond.

For all of Norah's capabilities, she was not familiar with changing a tire. Between her inexperience and Emery's useless arm, it took much longer than normally and dusk fell as Emery was tossing the jack back into the car. He took a look at the darkening sky and suddenly, he felt something of Norah's urgency. He slipped back into the passenger seat and when Norah looked at him, all he said was, "Hurry."

She did, speeding all the way into Deep Water. Later, when asked, Emery wouldn't have a clear answer as to why the gathering gloom was more ominous than usual. Dr. Skinner doubtlessly would have attributed it to exhaustion and their admittedly heightened state of nerves. But both Norah and Emery felt the same thing: something was wrong and they needed to get to the lake.

It was full on night by the time they arrived on the lake road and Norah's headlights lit upon Mr. Jensen's tall, thin figure, striding home confidently with his dog leading and his small son beside him. He stepped up cheerfully to Emery's door when Norah pulled to a halt.

"Evening, Norah, Chief," he said. "Stu and I are just coming back from your place."

"Is everything all right?" Norah asked anxiously.

"Appears to be."

"And Father?"

"Well, he called me this morning, must have been around eight."

"Eight!"

"He wanted help with the *Daisy Jane*, so the boys and I obliged him. He did a good job with the repairs. Course, she's still scarred."

"Did he say anything about what he was doing?"

"Told me and Tim he was doing some fishing, but that's it. When I went back there after your call, he'd taken Fido and the boat out. I suspect he wanted a little time on the water to clear his head. It's what he does when something's not right."

"I know," Norah said.

"Did you go inside?" Emery asked.

"Oh, sure," Jensen said. "We looked around, stood at the base of the stairs and shouted, but nothing. I'm sure he's all right, Norah. His doctor said that fishing is just the sort of thing he ought to do – relax and do what he loves, right?"

"Right," Norah said. Her hands gripped the steering wheel tightly.

Emery said, "We appreciate you checking in on him."

"What are neighbors for?" Jensen shrugged and

his curious gaze fell on the sling. "Looks like you two had an exciting day."

"And a long one," Emery admitted and forced a yawn. "Sorry to be rude, but..."

"Oh, sure, sure." Jensen, obviously disappointed, stepped back from the car door. "You all let me know if you need anything. We're right down the street."

"Thank you!" Norah called as she pulled away from the side of the road.

***

The house was dark and quiet as they pulled up into the driveway. Norah killed the engine and was out of the car almost before Emery was, but he caught up with her and grabbed her arm.

"Norah," he said quietly. "Why don't you let me go first?"

She shook her head. "I'll go with you," she said. "Right beside you."

He tucked her arm into his good one and they proceeded around the back.

The yard was still and sky clear enough that

crystal shafts of moonlight made the water sparkle like diamonds. Emery saw at once that Jensen was correct: the *Daisy Jane* was gone and there was no sign of Fido. The rowboat alone bumped up against the dock, empty and dark. Nevertheless, he led Norah around the back of the house and inside.

There was no sign of life in the house, either. The bottom floor was just as they left it, with the only immediately noticeable difference being that someone, presumably the captain, had rummaged through the kitchen cabinets.

"It looks like Jensen was right about the fishing trip," Emery said.

"I want to check his room," Norah said.

But it, too, bore the signs of departure. The bed was made and when Norah checked his closet, she reported that his fishing clothing was, indeed, gone.

"Why isn't he back yet?" she asked. She obsessively started tidying the already neat room, adjusting nick-nacks and refolding blankets. "Where can he be?"

Emery shifted his sore arm uncomfortably.

"Maybe he needed more time to think things through."

"What things? Wouldn't he want to know what happened to us? We didn't exactly tell him what was going on."

"I did."

She stopped her fidgeting and looked at him. "What did you tell him, Emery?"

Her tone was ice and suddenly, Emery was reminded of his first night in Deep Water and her warning: *"I won't let you call him crazy... He's my father. He's all I have. And I won't let him down."*

"I told him about Philip," he said.

"And? What did he say?"

"You asked me to find out the truth, Captain. You told me whatever it was, you'd accept it from me. Do you still intend to stand by that?"

"He didn't believe me. He kept insisting that his monster attacked you, that we had to find it and kill it. I told him what the doctor said, that guilt caused him to create a reality that absolved him from his guilt. That Philip took advantage of this and that he had nothing to worry about."

"You don't believe me. You never believed me."

"I never believed in fairy tales."

"What did he say to that, Emery? Tell me what he *said*?"

Her eyes were flashing with temper now. She moved slowly towards him, her hands fisted, her tone low and angry.

"Protecting her was the only reason I brought you here, Emery. And I'll ensure her happiness and safety if it's the last thing I do."

"He said he'd never kill himself, Norah. He promised me he'd never do that to you. That protecting you was all that mattered. That it was…" he swallowed through a dry mouth. "Protecting you was why he sent for me."

There was a long, long moment of silence as she processed this. Emery discovered that his heart was racing, that the very floor beneath his feet seemed ready to give way at any moment. It was if he and Norah had reached a breaking point and the next moment was going to determine the future of something very important. But what that was, he honestly didn't know.

Finally, he broke the silence, reaching out to

her with his good hand and saying, "Norah, he asked me…"

She interrupted, stepping away from his gesture. "He reached out to you for help! To tell him that he *wasn't* crazy!"

"He *is* deluded, he must be." His innate truthfulness made him waver.

She saw and pounced: "But what, Emery?"

"You don't believe me. You never believed me."

Ice shot through Emery's veins. He felt fear like he had never felt before, not even that morning, running through the streets after a goon with a gun.

Captain Donovan had never actually stopped believing in the malevolent creature. Now he believed that the creature was capable of attacking – and killing – Norah. He'd spent his life trying to shield his daughter from the evil and now it was here.

"Charles, what is it?"

"Protecting her was the only reason I brought you here, Emery…"

Emery had thought it odd that Donovan let them go after the thugs without any protest at all. A protective father would never allow his only daughter to involve herself in a gun fight. But he would let her go if he didn't believe the situation was that bad – if, for instance, he thought the greater danger was in the backyard.

"....I'll ensure her happiness and safety if it's the last thing I do."

Captain Donovan would never commit suicide. But he would sacrifice himself.

Norah's hand was on his good shoulder now, shaking him.

"Charles, you're scaring me!"

Her voice was high and frightened. He stared at her and tried to get the words out.

"You don't believe me. You never believed me."

Donovan is going after the creature.

"Char-" Norah's high-pitched pleading cut off mid-word as though choked. She froze, mouth open, hand on his shoulder. Every last ounce of color drained from her face. She looked for all the world like someone who'd seen a vision of hell.

Now it was Emery's turn to snap out of it. He reached out and grasped her shoulder, shaking her.

"Norah? Norah, what is it?"

She looked at him, eyes wide in terror.

"I *hear* him," she whispered in a tone that made the ice climb Emery's spine.

"Who? Who do you hear? The captain?" he asked, barely allowing himself to hope. For he heard nothing.

"No..." she whispered. "I hear him... It."

"Who? Who, Norah? Answer me!"

Her grip on his arm tightened and she looked at him now almost desperately.

"The creature, Charles. I hear the creature."

23

They raced outside. Clouds were already beginning to gather overhead and the air, which had been so still and peaceful only moments before, was starting to turn blustery. It was as though something had reached out and switched the night from clear to stormy. And Emery, pre-occupied as he was, was just beginning to understand why.

He ran to the end of the dock, heart pounding and eyes straining against the deepening darkness. The island was just a dark smudge on the water, indistinct as though the clouds had come especially to cover it. For all Emery knew, they had.

Norah clattered up behind him, breathless and desperate.

"Do you hear it?" she asked again, almost pleading. "Charles, can you hear it?"

"No. I don't."

Then, across the far waters, Fido began to bark a warning. As if on cue, a light, like the beam of a flashlight, bounced in and out of sight.

"But I do see that," Emery said.

Norah's hand was gripping his good arm now.

"The island," she gasped. "We have to get there."

"Do you have any more guns?" Emery asked.

"I think so…"

"Get them."

She ran back into the house. By the time she came back, Emery had retrieved his pistol from the car, found the oars in the shed and was waiting in the rowboat for her. The night had gotten darker, the water choppier. The wind whipped across Emery's face and tossed Norah's hair as she ran down the dock towards him, empty handed. Across the water and over the watery noise, Fido's bark grew deeper.

"Father's pistol is gone!" Norah said and hopped into the boat. Her head whipped suddenly in the direction of the island.

"You hear him?" Emery asked.

"He's getting closer and… angrier."

"Help me with the oars."

She slid onto the bench beside him and shoved the boat away from the dock. Together, they began to row, pulling deep into the choppy water, their back towards the island. At first, Emery's one-handed row was stronger than Norah's two handed one, but within three strokes, she was keeping up with him. The wind increased and grew icy cold. The sky darkened. The waves grew bigger, tossing their little boat around. Water spray soaked their clothes and streams of water poured down Emery's face. Fido's bark grew fainter as the storm intensified. Thunder rolled.

"Do you hear it?" Norah shouted.

"Thunder."

"No! *It.*"

Emery just kept rowing, craning his head around every so often to check their progress.

Damn you, Captain! Why didn't you leave us the boat with the engine?

He knew why, of course, and the thought made him work even harder. The water fought them for every inch, tossing them first one way, then another. Sweat trickled down Emery's side and his one arm ached. The boat rose and fell. Norah fell into him, nearly losing her oar and igniting a firestorm in his shoulder. She yelped apologies.

"Just *row*," he shouted back and then, over the storm, they heard a deep snapping sound.

It was the captain's pistol.

Together, they both bent over the oars and pressed on. The second shot went off just as they made it around the bend of the island.

The *Daisy Jane* was there, bouncing amid the waves, its bow loose and unmanned. Fido stood on the island's shore, running back and forth, barking like mad. As the waves pitched their rowboat up again, Emery caught a glimpse of the Captain, beating at the waves with his pistol.

"Keep rowing!" he shouted.

For once, the storm worked with them. A deep wave shifted them and they came alongside the *Daisy Jane* so quickly that Emery had to put the oar up to prevent them from crashing. He tossed the oar to Norah and without a word, grabbed the pitching side of the *Daisy Jane*.

"Charles!"

Norah's cry was almost lost in the wind. The roll

and pitch of the waves yanked the bow upwards and Emery went with it, using the momentum – and his sore arm – to propel himself into the fishing boat. He landed on the deck with a hard crash, knocking the breath out of him. Luckily, though, he landed on his good shoulder. As he pushed himself upwards, he looked towards the stern.

Captain Donovan stood at the stern, beating the waves that threatened to submerge his vessel. He had tied himself to the boat with a variety of lines, to prevent himself from going overboard, but the pitch of the waves and the water under foot were making him stagger for balance. His swings, too, were wild and rapidly losing energy and the roar of the wind was so bad that Emery could only tell that Donovan was screaming by the glimpses of the expression on his face.

Emery shouted uselessly into the wind as he regained his footing. Perhaps Donovan heard, because he stumbled back a half step and turned. Emery had one brief look at the man's gray face before Captain Donovan collapsed to the deck.

The water reached for him.

Hands like claws formed out of water, gripping

the stern. A head arose, a head that was half-man's, half-animal's, horned, evil, and almost translucent. It was bigger than a man and there was power in the way it pushed itself upwards, against the storm and the boat. As Emery watched, slack-jawed and unbelieving, the water-being rose over the stern like an avenging angel and opened its mouth to let loose a soul-tearing sound of remorse and revenge.

It reached for Donovan.

The pistol was already in Emery's hand, though he never could remember pulling it. He shouted and when the monster looked towards him, he fired, once, twice, three times. The monster cried out, the waves responded and the boat rose and dropped with the suddenness of a roller coaster. Emery's feet went out from under him and he hit the deck hard, losing his grip on the pistol. The prow of the ship tilted upward, sending him sliding towards the monster.

The monster reached for him with clawed hands. Emery twisted and turned his slide into a charge. He narrowly avoided the claws and hit the monster feet first. Though the being looked as though it were made of water, it felt like solid flesh and the impact of Emery's body was just enough to knock it off balance. It fell backwards into the water with a shriek of anger. As it fell, though, one claw snagged Emery's foot and pulled him in. Emery hit the railing first, and then went overboard.

Well-honed instincts kept Emery from gulping water. He plunged into the lake and immediately lost all sense of direction. Only the painful grip on his ankle anchored him to the reality of the fight. He began to kick and flail and at first was rewarded only by excruciating pain when the claw twisted. But then his free foot hit something solid and flesh. He kicked again and again, even as his lungs burned for air and darkness threatened to overwhelm him.

Suddenly, the grip on his ankle released and he was tossed away, like trash in the swirl of water and darkness. Now the darkness was not just around him, but overtaking him. His shoulder burned, his ankle was numb, and his muscles seemed to have lost all power. He had no sense of which way was up. His lungs were burning and he could see nothing. He kicked and pulled with his arms, but the exhaustion and pressure were overwhelming.

Then, just when he was about give up, something wrapped about his chest like an iron band and pulled. He fought weakly, panic almost breaking through his sluggish mentality, but the band was stronger than he. It wasn't until his head broke free of the water and air slapped him like a strong hand that he realized that the band was an arm and the arm belonged to Norah.

Instincts kicked in and he began to tread water. He coughed and choked. Norah was shouting something at him, but the wind was worse and the waves higher than before. He shook his eyes clear and turned towards her voice.

She was trying to swim against the waves, but the wind and the storm held her in place. She screamed again and he turned.

The *Daisy Jane* was bucking wildly in the storm. Emery could just barely make out the figure of the monster, the sea satyr, climbing the stern again, bigger than before and shimmering in the dim light. His wild roar overcame even wind. His broad back loomed up over the boat and Emery caught a flash of snapping claw.

"Father!" Norah screamed.

Emery tried to swim forward, but the water was relentless.

The monster roared in triumph again and bent over.

Norah screamed. Emery swam. The storm raged.

The monster bent... then staggered. His triumphant roar turned into a scream. He twisted and Emery saw the harpoon jutting out from his chest. As they watched, trying desperately to swim forward, the monster began to dissolve, as though the rain pouring down on it were acid. He arched in pain, claws desperately scrambling for the harpoon, but it was too late – it was too deep. With a final roar, the monster pitched over the side and disappeared in the water.

Emery turned back to look at Norah. Her eyes were wide, her face pale. She'd seen it too.

"Father!" she called and coughed when a wave smacked over her.

Emery turned and saw that there was a new figure standing at the stern of the boat.

Captain Donovan stood, gripping the rail and staring at the water. He was screaming into the darkness, but the storm and the thunder carried it away and they could hear nothing.

Epilogue

Later, when the *Daisy Jane* and the rowboat were safely tied up to the dock and they themselves were in dry clothes, the three sat around the dining room table, drinking hot coffee and trying to piece the world back together.

The storm had ended almost immediately with the creature's death and Donovan had recovered quickly, picking up both Norah and Emery in the *Daisy Jane*. Once on board, Norah had asked, "Was that... when Jasper...?"

"Yes," the captain had said. "It was the same creature." He looked as though he were about to go into mourning.

"Is it dead?"

"Yes. And there's no use in looking for a body."

Emery remembered that brief glimpse when the monster was writhing and its body was dissolving before their eyes, the death rattle in his cry, and the sharp plunge into the waters. They had no evidence except their own eye witness accounts and a few new claw marks on the railings. The nightmare was finally over.

Now they sat in the stillness of the lake house. The wound on Emery's ankle was nearly identical to Norah's and both of them sat with their ankles propped up on empty chairs. Donovan had seen to the bandages, including those on Emery's shoulder, and had made the coffee while they changed. Watching him now, Emery thought he looked like a new man. And why shouldn't he? He'd just reclaimed his sanity and slayed the beast that had held him in fear for so long. By all rights, he ought to be opening a bottle of champagne.

Yet there was a sobriety to the captain's carriage. He told them that the attack on Norah that morning had confirmed for him that he was not crazy, that there was a monster in the lake.

"He wanted revenge," Emery said. "He blamed you for the death of... her."

The captain nodded. "I guess I was at fault at that. At least partially. I might have given myself up to him. I was considering it. I couldn't stand the tension, the waiting. All these years of wondering and fear and then..."

"I understand him, you know," he said, looking

into his mug as though the answers to life's riddles were there. "I know what it's like to lose the woman you love. I know what it's like to have sorrow eat at you from the inside until all the world feels like it's in shadow. Grief can destroy you. It can make you destroy yourself. But I was never alone in my sorrow. I guess I was luckier than he was. So I was sympathetic. But when he attacked Norah this morning..."

He shivered and instinctually reached out for Norah. She took his hand and held it in both of her own. The look of understanding that passed between them was touching and Emery was surprised by how distant he suddenly felt.

"That changed things," Emery filled in, breaking the moment.

The captain nodded. "It was him or me then and he would not be satisfied with a substitute. That's why I didn't go with you this morning. I knew that I had to wait until nightfall and he would come for me." Suddenly, he grinned. "Of course, if I knew you were driving my daughter into a shoot-out, I might have had second thoughts."

"She did the driving, sir," Emery said. "I was just a passenger."

"Idiot," Norah said and shot him a smile that warmed Emery all the way through.

"I was hoping it would be done before you returned," Donovan said. "But I should have known you'd have my daughter home by curfew."

"Always, sir."

After a moment of silence, Norah asked, "What do we do now? Tell the police?"

"Tell them what?" Emery asked.

"We have to say something," she insisted. "They still think that Father is... We have to clear him somehow."

"That is going to be difficult."

Her dark eyes snapped with temper. "We all saw it!"

"Why would they believe us? Setting aside the fact that we are trying to convince Sheriff Young that evil mermen exist..."

"Sea satyr," Donovan interrupted.

"Setting the myth aside, everyone knows you'd go to almost any length to protect your father and I'm almost as bad. We'd never be believed, Norah. Not without proof. Not without a body."

"There must be something left," she said.

Donovan shook his head. "She dissolved

completely. He probably did the same. Our best bet would be to find another and how can we do that?"

She looked from one man to the other, disbelief writ large on her pale face. "So that's it? We just let them believe that my *father* is crazy? That's the end of the story?"

"We know, Norah," Emery said quietly. "That will have to do for now."

Norah turned her angry gaze from him towards her father. "Is that enough for you, Father?"

He nodded, resolute and certain. "It is more than I'd hoped for, Norah. More than I thought I deserved."

Relief fairly poured out of him. He'd really thought himself insane. Even his sending for Emery was merely a cry for help, for the courage to do what was necessary. Captain Donovan had given up on himself – and he'd been restored. Emery couldn't imagine the kind of mental torture the old man had endured the past few years, just as he couldn't imagine what it must be like to know, really know, that you were never crazy to begin with.

Out of force of habit, Emery disguised his quick prayer of thanksgiving with a sip of cool coffee.

Norah looked less than satisfied. She'd wanted nothing less than a full exoneration, but given a few days' reflection, she'd come to know what a true victory this really was. In time, she'd come to accept and even rejoice in it.

At the moment, though, she was not done.

"All right," she said, stiffly. "But what are we going to do about Philip?"

As if on cue, Emery's shoulder ached and Donovan's head dropped a half an inch.

"Poor Philip," he said sadly.

Norah snapped, "He tried to destroy you, Father. His own uncle and he would have had you committed!"

The captain nodded. "His cruelty comes from weakness and he was not the only man that thought I was insane. If it's revenge you want, Norah, Philip's own weakness will be his downfall. A gambling addiction is like a cancer and it will get him in the end. I will not add to it. I've caused enough pain."

Emery asked, "What will you do now, Captain?"

"I live again." Donovan looked around the room and sighed wistfully. "I will miss this place."

"You aren't leaving?" Norah asked, aghast.

In answer, Donovan stood and walked to the windowed doors that lead out to the patio. Outside, Deep Water Lake lay still and dark against the dark forested shoreline. The night was nearly gone and grey was creeping across the sky. Dawn was approaching and with it would come the early morning mists and the sound of the early birds.

Leaning one arm against the pane of glass, Donovan's low voice rumbled:

"I must go down to the seas again, to the lonely sea and the sky.

"And all I ask is a tall ship and a star to steer her by;

"And the wheel's kick and the wind's song and the white sail's shaking.

"And a grey mist on the sea's face, and a grey dawn breaking."

The words struck a chord deep within Emery and he found himself longing for the sea, the salt air and the rolling deck beneath his feet. He looked at Norah. She was looking at her father, her expression soft and her profile was lovely in that gentle light. He wondered if she ever longed for the sea. He wondered if she was the type who would remain on shore, waiting for the man who did.

As if she heard his thoughts, Norah said, "You're going back to the sea." It was a question as much as a statement and she turned back to Emery as though to include him in it.

"I must," Donovan said simply. "I was born for it and I gave it up far too easily. When a man – or a woman – has a call, they must follow it, or risk becoming an empty shell of themselves."

He turned back to the pair of them. His shoulders were back now and his head held high. He looked at his daughter with sympathy and assurance.

"This house was never really mine. There comes a time when a refuge turns into a prison. I've hidden for far too long. I must learn to face the world again. And you have to let me, Norah. You have your own life to live." His gaze shifted to Emery.

Emery kept his expression neutral and he refused to even glance at Norah. "Where will you go?"

"Back to Portsmouth. I still have friends there.

My old pal, Fred, offered me a charter cruise whenever I wanted it. It's kid's stuff, but it's a step in the right direction." He looked at Norah, who was studying her hands, then back to Emery. "And you?"

Emery looked at his mug. "I haven't quite decided," he said and felt more than saw Norah's gaze on his face. "I've been offered retirement or a teaching position. It would mean more time on shore, probably in Portsmouth, training cadets how not to run aground."

"Is that what you'd like to do?" Norah asked.

There was something in the tenor of her voice that made him look at her. There was something like a promise in the light of her eyes that made hope wash over Emery. He knew, beyond the shadow of a doubt, that he *did* have many useful years ahead. It was time for something new, something different, something that was quite possibly wonderful. The sea wasn't the only siren.

Norah was still waiting on his answer, so he said, "Not initially. But now... now it seems tempting. A man could grow an opportunity like that. Maybe settle down, start his own charter cruise business. Build a home. On land even. I don't know. It seems worth thinking about."

Norah's smile deepened.

"Yes, Chief," she said. "It does."

**BOOK ONE of
THE ENCOUNTER series:**
TALE HALF TOLD
1971

EXCERPT:

There was in the air a sense of impending battle. Johnny knew it like he knew the scent of napalm. The world was conspiring against them, gathering forces, preparing to strike. The wind was the first line, whipping up the light snow from the ground and sending it, stinging, into their faces as they struggled through the drifts towards the car. Johnny took the lead and Michael brought up the rear. It was not snowing yet, but Johnny could taste it in the air and he did not like it. The storm was moving much too fast.

He pulled open the passenger door and helped Linda in while Susan moved around the front of the vehicle towards her door. Michael stumbled next to him, fumbling for the handle.

"You're right," he said to Johnny, raising his voice to be heard above the wind. "Let's get out of here before a tree falls."

There was an audible sigh of relief when the doors were shut. After turning over twice, the engine started. Michael shifted into reverse and pulled backwards as the wind, roaring in defeat, slammed into the side of the car, causing the entire vehicle to shudder.

"Good grief!" Linda said. "What is with the weather today?"

No one answered her. Michael had gone too deep into the drifts behind them and was gently trying to ease the spinning tires back onto pavement. Susan looked ill again. Johnny found himself sitting at attention as though expecting an attack at any minute.

Stop it, he told himself, and then said aloud to Linda, "It's just the wind coming off the river, that's all. Want me to get out and push, Mike?"

Even as he said it, the tires caught traction and they began moving towards the road.

"We're on our way now," Michael said heartily. "Just a little bit of New England weather."

His white knuckle-hold on the constantly shifting steering wheel belied his confident tone. They knew better than to reply. Even the backseat passengers could feel the shift of the slipping tires while they were still on flat ground. All around them, the wind whipped up the sugar-like snow, casting drifts and fresh layers onto their path.

The driveway was only a few hundred yards long, ending in a sharp downslope to the road. Michael slowed as he reached it, until the tires caught ground and held.

"It's slippery," Susan warned.

Michael said, "I know, honey, I know," as he eased the car forward. They reached the lip of the incline and the car tipped.

"Easy does it..." Michael said, just before the tires touched ice.

The car hurtled down the slope, picking up speed and twisting as Michael fought for control. Johnny braced himself and reached out for Linda, who had one hand clasped to her mouth. Susan was climbing up into her seat, bracing her legs against the dashboard, repeatedly crying, "Michael, the tree! Michael, the *tree!*"

The car turned despite Michael's frantic struggle with the wheel and pounding on the brakes. They slipped down the end of the driveway, slid across the road and tipped over the edge into the ditch. Susan's scream was cut off abruptly when they hit the trees with a crescendo of breaking glass and the bone-crunching sound of metal wrapping around wood.

AVAILABLE NOW ON KINDLE AND IN PAPERBACK

Margaret Traynor and **Killarney Traynor** are sisters who live in New Hampshire and have way too much time on their hands. **Margaret** is an EA, travel enthusiast, and coffee fanatic who works in an accounting office during the day and hikes the White Mountains on the weekends. **Killarney** is an author, actress, and bookworm and generally too busy watching black and white movies to hike. *The Encounter Series* is founded in their mutual love of "The Twilight Zone", "X-Files", Agatha Christie, and Alfred Hitchcock.

For more information about *The Encounter Series,* visit www.KillarneyTraynor.com

The Encounter Series

Tale Half Told: 1971
Universal Threat: 1985
The Monster of Deep Water Lake: 1934

By Killarney Traynor:

Jenny Goodnight

The Mysteries Next-Door series
Summer Shadows
Necessary Evil
Michael Lawrence: the Season of Darkness